Gaia forced herself to stop reading for a moment. Her circulation was moving at light speed. It was too much to digest in one sitting. Too much reality flying off those old pages.

It dawned on Gaia that she was probably sitting in the *exact* spot where her mother had written these words. Her connection to Katia was suddenly something physical. Something palpable. Her eyes began to well up from the overflow of. . . something. Joy? Relief? Some kind of raw, unpurified emotion that she couldn't even name.

Don't miss any books in this thrilling series:

FEARLESS™

Available from SIMON PULSE

FEARLESS™

BEFORE GAIA

FRANCINE PASCAL

SIMON PULSE
New York   London   Toronto   Sydney   Singapore

First Simon Pulse edition July 2002

Text copyright © 2002 by Francine Pascal

Cover copyright © 2002 by 17th Street Productions, an Alloy, Inc. company.

SIMON PULSE
An imprint of Simon & Schuster Children's Publishing Division
1230 Avenue of the Americas, New York, NY 10020

Produced by 17th Street Productions,
an Alloy, Inc. company
151 West 26th Street
New York, NY 10001

Printed in the United States of America
10 9 8 7 6 5 4 3 2 1

This book has been catalogued with the Library of Congress.
ISBN: 0-689-85179-0

To Merry & Mort Young

She couldn't
believe
she'd let it
lie dormant
in her
psyche for **2002**
this long.
The dream
at the
monument. . .

GAIA MOORE WAS JUST ABOUT READY

to burn this day. As in torch it. As in press delete and erase it from memory. The entire day had been such an utter waste of time. She had already endured two inane arguments with two different teachers, three separate

Spot the redhead

comments from the insufferable Friends of Heather—two declaring a "frizz alert" on her hair and one insulting her "boy-band pants," whatever the hell that meant. And to top it all off, she had a noxious headache the size of Mount Vesuvius that was threatening to erupt at any second. Actually, to truly top it all off, there was the rest of Gaia's life. The tragic, all too melodramatic life that always bubbled and simmered just beneath the surface, forcing her to put on a "normal" face while tiny bits of her sanity slowly chipped away and fell into the burning pit of her stomach.

Perhaps she was feeling a tad too dramatic today.

But still, she might have managed to make it home from school without completely losing it, were it not for that one rude son of a bitch—who could break the will of even the most hardened New Yorker. He was a member of that despicable club of citizens Gaia generally referred to as the *urban tacklers*.

Urban tacklers: those disgruntled boobs of the

masses who rammed right into you on the street for no apparent reason, knocking you and your knapsack or your bag of groceries down to the ground and then moving on as if nothing at all had happened.

Gaia had always prided herself on seeing potential urban tacklers coming down the street. That idiot with a Swiss watch and a briefcase who couldn't bother to look where he was going or that eight-foot-tall anorexic model who just *had* to make it to her shoot on time, even if it meant flattening some poor sucker standing between her and the cover of *New York Bitch* magazine. Usually Gaia was able to dodge them or else give them a slight elbow to the shoulder, sending them off in the other direction like oversized metropolitan pinballs. But today she just hadn't been prepared.

"Oompf!" She coughed up every ounce of air in her lungs as this freight train of a man bashed her in the gut and ran her over without a single word of apology, without even breaking his stride for a moment. The apparent master of human hit-and-runs was already halfway down the block when Gaia found herself lying flat on the sidewalk, her book bag two feet ahead of her and her headache magnified by a thousand. She leapt back to her feet and swiped her bag up off the ground, giving his back the look of death. Man, was she aching to release some of today's pent-up frustration.

"Hey!" she growled, trying to get a better look at her assailant as he neared the other corner. With his back to her, all she could see was a thin layer of graying red hair on his head and one of those old tweed sport jackets with the fake suede patches on the elbows. For an old man, he'd knocked her down with one hell of a wallop. Old or not, he still deserved a piece of Gaia's mind.

She broke into a full run, nearly catching up with him. But when she turned the corner to follow him. . . he was gone. Nothing but a mass of Chanel-wearing mothers in oversized sunglasses.

He had literally disappeared.

Gaia slammed her book bag to the ground, picked it up, and then slammed it to the ground again. There was no worse sensation than the feeling of having someone knock you down in the street and then escape, leaving you completely *unavenged*—leaving you with nothing to do but stew in your own failure and powerlessness. She was just about ready to start pounding her own head against the building on the corner of Seventy-second and Madison when she realized. . .

There was something poking at her chest. Something had been stuffed in the inside pocket of her jacket. And it had not been there a minute before.

She reached under her coat and pulled out an envelope. One small tattered envelope. *For Gaia Moore*, it read, almost illegibly. She stared blankly at her name as her mind caught up with her rash emotions.

Wake up, Gaia. This little collision had nothing to do

with street politics or having a lousy day. It hadn't been some random crash in the street. It wasn't an urban tackle at all. Gaia knew enough about espionage tactics to realize what had just happened. She had just been "contacted."

IT WAS ONE OF THE OLDEST TRICKS

Count Chocula

in the book. The "bump and run" or the "give and go"—probably one of the first methods of contact her father had ever taught her. When an agent needed to make contact without being spotted, this was often the cleanest method. One quick bump on the street and a message could be delivered without any detection by surveillance. Sometimes without the recipient even knowing she had received it.

Gaia darted her head from corner to corner of Madison Avenue, hoping she might spot the redhead again. But it was no use. He'd blended into the crowd within seconds of message delivery.

She turned her attention back to the envelope, staring one last time at her name in an alien scrawl before ripping it open like a starving child who'd just found the last Hershey bar on earth. She stuffed her fingers in and pulled out a medium-size postcard.

That was all that was inside. One postcard.

And the moment she saw the picture on the front cover. . . she felt dizzying waves of nausea overtake her entire body. She was staring at one of her least-favorite places in all of New York City. The Soldiers' and Sailors' Monument.

The Soldiers' and Sailors' Monument was a towering white stone memorial and an expansive concourse built on the edge of Manhattan's Upper West Side, right by the Hudson River. It had been built years ago to honor all the soldiers and sailors who had died fighting the Civil War. Certainly a noble reason to erect a monument. Still, Gaia had always loathed that monument and the entire concourse surrounding it. She detested it almost irrationally, as if she had more reasons to hate it than she even knew or understood.

She had a faint memory of her father taking her there when she was a little kid. He would pick her up from her first-grade class, take her down to Soldiers' and Sailors' for a quick combat training session, and then drop her back off at school before lunchtime was over. God, how she'd hated every one of those lessons. Though that made absolutely no sense. She'd always loved training sessions with her father. What was it about those sessions that she hated so much?

That was the most disturbing thing of all. The *not* remembering. Her photographic memory never failed her. It was one of her many unexplainable gifts.

Think, Gaia. What's the matter with you? Try to remember. Something. Anything. . .

She used to believe that the entire monument was still a dangerous war zone—that perhaps in the middle of the night, when all the New Yorkers had gone to sleep, full-fledged battles still took place on that concourse, replete with charging armies and explosive gunfire, blood-soaked bodies, and severed limbs.

Blood-soaked bodies. . .

Suddenly she was struck with an image of a blood-soaked man in a black cotton suit. He had a tortured expression on his face—some horrid combination of disbelief and anguish. Who was that man? Who the hell was she picturing?

And then it hit her. Though she almost wished it hadn't. Her father. It was a memory of her father standing by the monument, covered in blood. But a moment more and she realized. . . this was not an actual event she was remembering. This was a nightmare. A very, very old recurring nightmare.

God. That dream. How could I ever forget that horrible dream?

It had haunted her every other night for close to a year when she was ten years old. The same nightmare again and again. She couldn't believe she'd let it lie dormant in her psyche for this long. The dream at the monument. . .

It was always the exact same sequence of surreal events:

Her father is standing in the middle of the concourse,

7

wearing one of his black tailored suits. In his hand he holds a gun, but he's not aiming it outward. He has turned it toward himself.

Gaia is a few feet away from him. She is no older than five or six, dressed in her bright purple sweatshirt and matching corduroys, screaming desperately for her father to put down the gun. But her screams are ignored. Her mother is there, too, standing only inches from her father, also screaming.

Ear-shattering explosions go off all around them, from every side of the monument. Shots rain down on them from the Hudson River. It's a war—a modern-day Civil War—and Gaia's family is stuck in the center of the battle. Gaia struggles to get to her father before he can fire the gun at himself, but she's immobilized. She can't move forward no matter how violently she struggles, no matter how loudly she screams.

And then he fires. He fires bullets into his own body. His shots can barely be heard over the din of the battle as holes erupt all over his chest and arms, dark red blood shooting out of his gaping wounds in ugly rhythmic spurts. . . .

And that was always as far as she'd gotten in the dream. She'd wake up before she could stop him from killing himself.

But this line of thinking would get her absolutely nowhere. She forced herself to shake off all those loathsome memories. This mystery agent had to have had more in mind than just pissing Gaia off and sending her down a very ugly memory lane.

She flipped the postcard over. A typewritten note was folded up and taped to the back side of it. She ripped it off the card, darting her eyes right and left for surveillance as she stepped back into the shadows of the corner building. She unfolded the yellowing piece of paper, desperate to devour every word that her mysterious urban tackler had written.

Gaia,

Do you remember this monument? It was the only time you and I ever met. Perhaps you've forgotten. You were quite young. If I'd seen what you saw at that age, I probably wouldn't want to remember it, either. It's better if you don't remember me, anyway.

There is very little you need to know about me. I don't work for your father, and I don't work for your uncle. Not anymore. I am doing this for my own reasons. I am doing this because I am old. Too old. And if you have lived a life like mine, then all you have left in your old age is regret. Regret for all the heartless, selfish things you have done.

My greatest regret is what I have done to you, Gaia.

Gaia, listen to me now. This is what you must

understand. Loki has been confusing you and manipulating you with nothing but lies and half-truths for so long. That is why I have contacted you.

I am here to give you the truth, Gaia. I know that "truth" has become a very relative term for you. So I have brought proof.

Proof of your past in every possible form. My organization (or rather, the one I belonged to until today) deals in information. It is an organization far more powerful and resourceful than the CIA, and let's just say that I have "permanently borrowed" a number of very valuable files from our headquarters. I am now in possession of not only extensive photos, but also just about every piece of personal documentation pertaining to your family and your past. I have dossiers on you, your father, your uncle, even your mother. So you see, I will not need to convince you of any stories. I will simply provide you with all of this documentation—the clues. All you need to do is put the clues together, and you will learn the entire truth for yourself.

Of course, Loki has surely learned of the missing dossiers by now, and I'm quite sure that I have been slated for termination. But Loki cannot kill me if he cannot find me. So, we must do this my way. The rules are unfortunate, but they are absolute necessities:

1. I cannot be seen, and we cannot be seen together.
2. I must stay constantly mobile.
3. I can only provide you with clues that can be carried and hidden quickly.

Once I am absolutely sure that I have shaken Loki's surveillance, I will inform you of a meeting place where I'll be able to provide all the remaining materials and answers you need in full detail. But for now, we must proceed with extreme caution.

If you agree to my terms, then signal me by following up on the first clue. The choice is yours. I will wait for your answer.

Let me give you your past so you can change your future. As George Santayana once said, "Those who cannot remember the past are condemned to repeat it."

THAT WAS IT. NO SIGNATURE, NO

Sherlock Holmes

further explanation, nothing. The only other thing on the page was an illegible scribble at the bottom.

The note had momentarily overloaded Gaia's brain. Was any

of this for real? What did he mean, "It was the only time you and I ever met"? Who was he? And if Gaia *had* met him, then why on earth couldn't she remember?

She slid down against the wall of the building, staring at the note in one hand and the disturbing postcard in the other. This mystery agent somehow seemed to understand her better than her father did. But what struck her even more than his understanding of her botched life was his damn near clairvoyant understanding of the cure. He was absolutely right. The only thing that could heal her now, the only thing she still allowed herself to yearn for, was the truth about her past. Maybe she could understand her mother. She had lost her so young that sometimes, no matter how much she loved her, she wasn't sure whether she'd really known the woman at all. And she had already heard so many different stories, so many broken shards of history that never fit together. Maybe the mystery agent could finally help her to sift out the lies and put all those broken pieces together. Maybe he could tell her once and for all how everything went so terribly wrong with her parents and her uncle. Maybe he could finally tell her who the *real* Loki was, her uncle or her father? And God willing, maybe he could tell her, definitively and unequivocally, *whether her fearlessness was engineered or just a freakish accident of nature.*

The mystery agent held so many potential answers. Could he be just another unreliable manipulator like her uncle and her father? Was this just another one of Loki's tricks? Was he there only to confuse her and fill her head with more truckloads of horse crap?

But he'd already answered that question, hadn't he? She didn't need to trust him. All she needed to do was examine his supposed files full of evidence. And the sooner she saw his "evidence," the sooner she'd know whether he was a friend or a foe, whether his version of history was fact or fiction.

Good. Fine. Then it was decided. Gaia was in. She was in one hundred percent.

All she had to do was find the first clue. Which apparently was easier said than done.

She scanned every one of the sentences in his note. Maybe there was some kind of code embedded in his words. . . .

Then she scanned the postcard itself, scouring over the picture again and the blank white space on the other side, but she found nothing.

Jesus, was he trying to avoid Loki's surveillance or was this supposed to be some kind of ridiculous treasure hunt? Gaia was in no mood to play Sherlock Holmes. She ran through the note again until she had the ingenious idea to *turn the note over.*

When she saw the flip side of the note, she realized that he had not typed it on a regular piece of blank paper. He had typed it on the back of a title page from an old book. No wonder the paper was so thin and yellowed with age. It had been ripped out of a book that was probably more than twenty years old.

She examined the book's title, printed in bold elegant letters on the center of the page:

The History of the Peloponnesian War
Thucydides

Up in the top-right corner were her father's name and the date, written neatly in his unmistakable handwriting. *Tom Moore 2/15/83.* The bottom of the page had been stamped by the bookstore in blurry black ink.

Waverly Bookshop
16 Waverly Place

February 15, 1983. There was something special about that date—something her father had always. . .

Of course. The book. Gaia was suddenly awestruck by the weathered page in her hand. She'd known there was something special about this book, and now she finally understood what it was. This was the book her father had been searching for the day he met her mother. . . .

"The story of how young Tom met the even younger Katia," as her father used to say. He had told Gaia the story more than a few times.

It was a cold day in February 1983. He was searching for a book for his thesis—a rare edition of none other than *Thucydides*—and walked into this little bookshop on Waverly. That's when he first saw Gaia's mother, sitting on the floor of the bookstore, surrounded by stacks of books. As the story went, all it took was for their eyes to meet and they fell in love at first sight.

For a long time Gaia believed that she would fall in love just as quickly and as simply as her parents had. That was until she got older and found out that love felt less like the story her father told and more like a story from the Bible: lots of struggles and plagues—everyone either gets punished or dies. At least in her experience. All the more reason to envy and worship her parents' perfect love affair.

Suddenly this yellowed piece of paper had become incredibly precious to her. A page from the book that had brought her parents together. She ran the tip of her index finger gently across her father's signature, realizing how long ago he had written it. Long before Gaia had been loaded up with heinous resentment for him. More than a year before she had even been born. Long before everything had gone so terribly and miserably wrong.

Now she understood. The mystery agent was starting her off from the very beginning. From the very first day her parents had met. And this was his first "clue." Her heartbeat increased at an exponential rate as her eyes drifted down to the blurry stamp at the bottom of the page. The Waverly Bookshop. 16 Waverly Place.

Next stop: Greenwich Village.

WHAT IF IT WAS GONE?

This thought hadn't even occurred to Gaia until she'd jumped off the train at Sheridan Square. Her parents had met almost twenty years ago. What were the odds of some tiny cluttered bookshop still being at 16 Waverly?

History Repeating Itself

But as she raced down the quaint little street, with its well-preserved brownstones and its well-kept trees, she discovered a tiny glass blip in her peripheral vision. She nearly fell over, slamming on her own brakes. There on her right, squeezed mercilessly between two dark town houses, down a flight of gray iron steps to the basement level, was the Waverly Bookshop. It was hidden almost completely from view by the garbage cans on the landing and the stacks of dark, aging books filling up the glass window, but it was still there.

Gaia took the iron steps in one leap and tumbled into the shop, pushing the door against a rusty jingling bell that announced her entrance.

So this was where her parents had met. . . . To call the shop tiny would be a little too generous. It was a shoe box.

Peering over one of the towers of books, she could see the white-haired head of the proprietor.

"Afternoon," she heard him mutter.

"Hi," Gaia replied, standing up on her tiptoes to see the man's face. "Where's the history section?"

"You're looking at it," he mumbled, keeping his eyes pinned to his own book as he turned the dusty page.

"Riiight," Gaia replied, looking back toward the wall at a sea of unmarked shelves. "Um. . ." she began again, wondering if he would even answer two questions in a row, "do you have *The History of the Peloponnesian War*, by Thucydides?"

The old man's eyes actually drifted up from his book. He stared at Gaia over the top of his glasses, which were just about to fall off the edge of his nose. "Huh. . ." he grunted quizzically. "You know, I just had someone in here yesterday, sold me a rare edition of Thucydides. Isn't that amazing. . . ? Not worth anything, though. It's missing the title page."

Gaia tried not to swallow her tongue with excitement. She'd picked the right clue. "Where?" she blurted, knocking two books off a stack as she leaned forward. So much for containing herself. "Where is it?"

"Third shelf up on the wall behind you," he said.

She turned to survey the shelf. "Therman, Thilson, Thorn. . . Thucydides!"

She tugged the book out and dropped into a seated position against the shelf, flipping open the front cover. There was a thin strip of torn jagged paper close to the binding. She pulled the mystery agent's note out of her bag and placed it up against the tear. The edges matched perfectly. The page had definitely been ripped out of the front of this very book. Her heart skipped as she flipped to the next page. There was a quote printed at its center.

"History repeats itself. . . ."
—*Thucydides*

Again, this thing about history repeating itself. Just like the quote in his note. What was he trying to tell her? Was this supposed to be another clue? She flipped quickly through the book, looking for any other clues or clarifications, but there was nothing. If Gaia was expected to start reading through Thucydides, she would just have to shoot herself right now. She dropped the book to the floor with frustration.

But as she leaned to pick it up, she caught a glimpse of the shelf again. And that was when she saw it. There in the empty space where the book had been, peeking out from *behind* the row of books, was a large manila envelope.

She took out the thick padded envelope with her name once again scrawled in the center in red ballpoint ink and ripped open the top of the envelope. A small stack of handwritten pages fell into her lap.

The most gorgeous and familiar scent floated up from the parchmentlike pages. A scent that had always intoxicated her and comforted her, like rich and spicy lilacs. It was the smell of coming home after school. A real home. A home with her mother in it.

Gaia grasped the pages gently and brought them closer, letting the light shine on the smooth script handwriting. The words were written in Russian. And the handwriting was her mother's.

Unbelievable. Somehow the mystery agent had gotten possession of authentic pages from her mother's *journal*—her own private diary.

Gaia had always taken for granted that she was fluent in most of the modern languages, but at this moment she had never been so grateful for her extraordinary skills. Her mother's own private thoughts were sitting right before her eyes. . . and Gaia could translate every word.

The date on the first page: February 15, 1983.

2/15/83

I wish I could find the words to describe the beauty of a glazed chocolate doughnut. I just ate two of them in about four minutes. Perhaps I have found my justification for coming to this country—Dunkin' Donuts. The man who invented Dunkin' Donuts should be given some kind of national award for luring impressionable young women from communist countries over to the great United States. I am not here for political asylum, Mr. President. I am here for the doughnuts. It is not your free-trade economy that interests me. It is your use of rainbow sprinkles.

I wonder how much more time I'll spend alone in bookstores, "studying up" for a nonexistent journalism career. I mean, for God's sake, that was the reason I came to this country. Free speech. That and the whole horrible mess back home. But I don't know anymore about journalism — too dangerous in Russia, too uninspired here. If only my singing career would take off and I could put my dreams of becoming a journalist aside. Or maybe doughnuts are the answer. . . . Maybe I'll just be known as the Russian runaway who beat the doughnut-eating world's record in 1983.

I'm beginning to sound just like my mother. <u>negative</u>. I can't help it. It wouldn't be nearly as difficult if I weren't so alone. I don't understand it.

Where on earth are the quality men in this country? The ones with ideas and humor and. . . all right, at this point I'd settle for one without that horrible hairstyle worn by that poor guy from Flock of Seagulls. . . .

And why are all these Russian men coming on to me lately? There have been five or six in the past two months or so. It's so bizarre.

And even as I write this, <u>another one</u> has approached me. Another dim-witted Russian buffoon whom I have been ignoring for the last twenty minutes. He just pretends to look at books and then tries another line every few minutes. He's already attempted such brilliant openers as, "That's a lot of books you've got there," and, "I've never seen a woman read so many books." "Hmmm, that's funny," I want to say. "I've never seen a man with so few redeeming qualities." But that would only encourage him.

Oh my God. Never mind the nitwit who won't stop buzzing in my ear. The most beautiful man in New York City just walked in. Listen to you, Katia. You sound like an overexcited teenager.

Perhaps that's because you <u>are</u> an overexcited teenager. Now, get your heart out of your throat and breathe. Don't you look up and stare at him again.

No, I'm sorry. I have to look up and stare at him again.

GAIA FORCED HERSELF TO STOP

reading for a moment. Her
circulation was moving at light
speed. It was too much to digest
in one sitting. Too much reality
flying off those old pages.

Too Much Reality

It dawned on Gaia that she
was probably sitting in the *exact*
spot where her mother had written these words. Her connection to Katia was suddenly something physical.
Something palpable. Her eyes began to well up from the
overflow of. . . something. Joy? Relief? Some kind of raw,
unpurified emotion that she couldn't even name.

In fact, all these shapeless, overwhelming emotions
were really just the by-products of one very simple revelation. For the first time in her life, Gaia had realized that
her mother. . . the person she admired more than any
other and contemplated more than any other. . . was *just
like her.* The same attitude, the same frustrating combination of independence and loneliness, the same profound
appreciation for the glazed chocolate doughnut. Gaia and
her mother were related by more than just blood. And
somehow, at least for one moment, that had made everything—Gaia's past and present—so much lighter.

But that one revelation was just the beginning. She
peered down at the thick manila envelope and realized
that there was much more inside than just her
mother's journal pages.

She grabbed the open envelope and flipped it upside down as a veritable treasure trove of historical documentation fell into her lap. Leaning forward, she organized the remaining contents of the envelope: one fully equipped minidisc player, one blue binder, which she immediately recognized as a CIA transcript, and one minidisc. The disc was clearly meant to accompany the transcript and was titled:

Thomas Moore Incident Report—10/16/1990
CIA File # NIR-P4855J
Digital Transfer

The first voice she heard she couldn't recognize. The second voice sounded like a younger George Niven; she just wasn't sure. But the moment she heard her father's voice through the earphones, she knew the mystery agent was absolutely for real.

CIA File # NIR-P4855J *[Incident Report]*
Rating: *CLASSIFIED*
Transcript Recorded—10/16/1990 16:55:57
Administrating: Agent John M. Kent
Reporting: Agent Thomas Moore

AGENT KENT: Incident report, October 16, 1990, approximately 1700 hours. This is Agent John Kent administering, Agents Moore and Niven reporting.

KENT: Tom, if you'd like a little more time. . .

MOORE: No, John. I'm ready to report.

KENT: All right, then. If you wouldn't mind, based on today's unexpected events, the Agency would like you to start with February 15, 1983.

MOORE: The day I met her.

KENT: Yes. If you wouldn't mind.

MOORE: Mind? I could never mind talking about that day.

They could
have been
talking
about farm
equipment,
and it
would have
been just as
arrestingly
intense.

TOM STOOD ON THE CORNER OF

Waverly and Sixth Avenue and double-checked the address on the business card. *16 Waverly.* Where on earth was 16 Waverly? He'd walked down Waverly Place hundreds of times before, and there was no Waverly Bookshop, he was sure of it. He scanned an entire 360-degree radius and forced himself to walk east. *Tick-tock, Tom. Wasting time. . .*

Dudley Do-Right student

This was simply not what he should be doing, and he knew it. No offense to the academic community, but Tom's knowledge of history and historiography had already surpassed that of most of his professors, and the thought of having to defend his thesis to those hypocritical nimrods was wearing extremely thin. He had already suffered through two inane arguments this morning with two different professors who'd failed to credit him in recent publications, and it was all getting so pointless. So painstakingly tedious. *Such a waste of time.*

No. . . that wasn't it. That wasn't it at all. *Never lie, Tom. Especially not to yourself.* The truth was, his frustration had nothing to do with his professors. The only person he was truly frustrated with was himself.

The complete paralysis of Tom's life was no one's fault but his own.

Fact: His brother was already a full-fledged agent, and they were the exact same age. They were *twins,* for God's sake, so what the hell was Tom's problem? That was the question. They were supposed to be working together—Tom and Oliver, in the Agency, *together.* That had always been the plan. But here Tom was, looking for some obscure book for a useless graduate thesis, while Oliver was already out there on the front lines doing the one and only thing Tom wanted to do. The thing he was born to do: *be* an agent. He knew it with every ounce of his being, even if Agent Rodriguez couldn't see it. Which, obviously, he couldn't.

The thing was, as far as Tom was concerned, he was already an agent. He dressed like an agent: suits that blended into the background. He stayed fit like an agent: three hours a day of martial arts training (karate, jujitsu, aikido, t'ai chi, muay thai). He studied like an agent: modern and ancient languages, international policy, mathematical properties, encoding and code breaking. But most important, he had trained himself to *think* like an agent.

It was a skill—a trick he did with his eyes. He could look everywhere, notice everything, and people couldn't see him doing it. He could walk down Waverly Place right now, pissed and frustrated as hell, yet still looking like nothing other than a young fresh-faced kid, drinking in the clear winter air without a care in the world. But he was actually seeing everything. The car with the missing hubcap. The license plate of that car (Connecticut; badly bolted in). The woman shivering slightly in the cement doorway of the shabby apartment building. She was waiting for someone. He could tell by the anxious wrinkles in her forehead and the way she flicked her cigarette. She'd never remember seeing Tom, but two days from now, he would still remember her. That was the art of spying. And Tom had damn near mastered it, whether Rodriguez understood that or not.

God, who am I kidding? Tom scolded himself. *That's just a game. I'm just playing a kid's game.* He could play "spy boy" to his heart's content, but it would do nothing to mask the simple truth.

He was, in fact, *so* green that he'd nearly walked right by the Waverly Bookshop twice. *Oh, yeah, Tommy. You've mastered the art, all right.* Yes, the bookstore did in fact exist, though in Tom's defense, situated on the basement level, blocked off by garbage cans on the landing and featuring a dirty glass window, it would be easily missed by anyone.

Tom froze on the landing. He'd trudged down all this way just to get this one book, but now that he'd finally reached his pointless destination. . . he wasn't even sure he wanted to go in. Did he really want yet *another* book for a thesis he didn't even want to finish? A book recommended to him by an agent who thought he was nothing more than an eggheaded academic? No. No, he certainly did not.

But he did it, anyway, of course. . . because, God help him, Tom *was* Dudley Do-Right. Whether he wanted to be or not. *Duty bound,* or something like that. *Boring,* in other words. And so, consigned to a life of banality and excessive morality, he opened the next boring door in his boring life. . .

And then he saw her.

She was the very first thing he saw as he cracked open the door to the bookstore. And she was not boring. God, whoever she was, she was *so very far* from boring. The moment he saw this unearthly, stunning, exquisite stranger, she happened to turn up and look at him, too. And when her eyes accidentally met his, he could swear he actually heard a bell ring. *Was that the bell on the door, or. . . ?*

And then everything just stopped. Everything. His heart, his mind, time. . . they all stopped.

Say something, Tom, he hollered inside his head. *You're gawking, for God's sake. When have you ever had trouble talking to a beautiful woman? Speeeaak!*

Nothing. Not a word. The moment was still on pause. No, not even pause. It really had come to a full and complete stop. In fact, as far as Tom could tell, once he'd locked eyes with this beautiful creature, his *entire life* had stopped—the life he'd been living up until this point.

And a new one had just started.

YES, TOM WAS FROZEN AGAIN. HE wasn't at all easily shocked, but today he'd just been blown away twice in only a matter of seconds. First by her eyes, and now by this man's recognizable face.

Suede Elbow Patches

Him. The man from the picture Tom had glimpsed less than an hour ago.

What was his name? *Nicholas. . . ?* No. *Nikolai.*

His features were unmistakable: that bright red hair and pale white skin, that long crooked nose, the pristine tweed jacket with the suede elbow patches. Was he KGB? Wasn't that what Tom had overheard earlier? And now, after another moment to think about it, wasn't that just a little bit *too much* of a coincidence? That Tom would find Nikolai, a likely KGB agent, at this very bookstore at this very moment? There were obviously some things going on here that Tom didn't understand.

But now was not the time to think about that. If Nikolai was in fact KGB, that meant he was dangerous. How dangerous, Tom couldn't possibly know. But in matters of espionage, it was always best to assume the worst—that's what all the books said. So Tom did his best to become invisible again, watching Nikolai and the beautiful stranger in that way he had trained himself to do—without actually looking. . . .

"So you don't want to talk to me, I think," Nikolai said, looking down at her with his own pathetic version of a "sly" smile. His voice was deep, with a thick Russian accent.

No, Tom thought, keeping his profile to them as he pulled a book from the shelf and pretended to read. *No, she doesn't want to talk to you, you idiot. Maybe it's time for you to go.*

"What's the matter?" Nikolai asked, his voice turning disgustingly nasal as he stepped closer to her and leaned against her bookshelf, posing in his own tragically out-of-date "swinging guy" stance. "You don't like Russian guys, maybe? *Big* mistake. Russian guys. . . we *know* things, uh? We know what women *want*, you know? The secrets are passed down through the generations."

Then he reached out his hand, wrapped his fingers around her chin, and tried to turn her face toward his.

And that's when Tom broke—the moment Nikolai's disgusting hand touched her face. Tom slammed his book shut, dropped it to the floor, and stepped over to Nikolai, standing much too close to him.

"Okay," he spat out emphatically, smiling slightly to cap his overflowing frustration and disdain. "You know, in America, we don't *touch* women unless they *want* us to."

Nikolai froze momentarily. And in that silent blip of a moment Tom had the sharpest, most vivid sinking feeling that he never should have opened his mouth—that he'd just dropped himself into something very, very far over his head. But he didn't care. Not right now. Right now, all he cared about was that Nikolai remove his hand from the girl's face—the girl, who was now staring wide-eyed at Tom with an expression he couldn't possibly read.

And Nikolai did remove his hand. But he then gave Tom, a look that threatened to tear his heart directly from his chest. It was, without question, the darkest, coldest, most condescending glare Tom had ever seen. *"Don't talk to me,"* Nikolai said, with a deep, steady tone that sounded more like a grave warning than an insult.

Tom knew he couldn't bully Nikolai out of there. Not without using a totally inappropriate karate chop. But Tom had quickly devised a plan that would send Nikolai running from that bookstore without a single punch thrown.

"You know what?" Tom began, trying to lighten the tone between them. "Is that the history section behind you?"

"What are you talking about?" Nikolai mumbled with frustration, glancing briefly behind him.

"I'm talking about books," Tom replied with a smile. "This *is* a bookstore, right? I just need a book from the history section behind you."

Tom simply shoved himself between Nikolai and the girl, "accidentally" bumping Nikolai about three feet back as he examined the bookshelf behind them. Nikolai stumbled backward and nearly lost his balance.

"Look, you little punk," Nikolai menaced, trying to

get in Tom's face. "Go find your stupid little book some-where else, you understand? Don't make me *angry*."

"Just a *second*," Tom insisted, scanning across the shelves intensely.

This can work, Tom told himself, *I know this will work. Be an agent, Tom. You want to be someone's hero, then* be one.

"I know the book is here," Tom said, ignoring Nikolai's enraged eyes. "See, I'm a history major, and I'm looking for this book by Mussolini's foreign minis-ter, Gian Galeazzo Ciano. I'm sure it's here. I'm sure of it. Let's see, Ciano. . . Ciano. . ." Tom began to spell the author's name aloud as he searched the shelf ever so slowly. "C. . . C-i. . . Damn, I know it's here somewhere. . . . C. . . i. . . a. . . Still can't find it. . . C. . . i. . . a. . ."

Tom peeked over at Nikolai again. And his face had most definitely begun to change. The more he listened to Tom search for the book, the more concerned he looked. He was getting Tom's message. He was defi-nitely getting his message.

"What are you trying to. . . ?" Nikolai began.

"Ah, here it is!" Tom announced, pulling a Ciano book from the history shelf. "See, I knew it was behind you," he said, shoving the book in Nikolai's face. "*I knew the* C-I-A *was right behind you.*"

Tom stared coldly and deliberately into Nikolai's eyes. He wanted to be sure Nikolai understood his threatening message. And judging from Nikolai's

33

sudden silence, he had. The slightest hint of paranoia suddenly spread across Nikolai's face as his eyes darted from side to side, and he even turned to look slightly behind him. He was now wondering if the CIA was, in fact, right behind him—if they were perhaps watching him from all sides at this very moment, observing him. Or perhaps. . . perhaps the CIA was standing right in *front* of him? In the form of a twenty-three-year-old grad school student. Of course, that was only true in Tom's dreams, but Nikolai didn't know that, did he? He didn't know anything anymore. Yes, Tom's little encoded message had him completely spooked.

"Maybe you should go now," Tom stated, keeping his eyes locked with Nikolai's.

Nikolai was dead silent. He tried to give Tom one last menacing glance, but his eyes were already darting toward the door. If the CIA was in the vicinity, then Nikolai needed to be gone. All he had left to offer Tom was a small piglike grunt. He looked down at the girl one last time, and then he turned around and walked himself out of the bookstore.

Tom had won. He had just won a showdown with a likely KGB agent. Now if he could just open his mouth and *talk* to her. Or perhaps, just maybe, she could say something to *him?* Something along the lines of, "My hero," perhaps? Maybe a nice little, "Thanks for sticking up for me. . . ?"

But she said nothing of the kind. Instead she stared

at him for another long beat, seeming to examine every aspect of his body and his face. And then she finally spoke to him.

"Why didn't you just kick his ass?" she asked in an elegant Russian accent.

Tom was speechless. Completely and utterly speechless. He was also rather sure that he had just fallen in love.

Face to Face

TONE IT DOWN, KATIA. THIS ONE *doesn't deserve it.*

Why did she always have to do this? Why did she have to tease them when she liked them? What was she, *five years old?* She might as well have pulled his hair or stolen his graham crackers and apple juice.

She picked herself up from the floor, being sure not to leave her journal behind. The last thing she needed was for him to accidentally see the embarrassingly adolescent things she'd been writing about him while that redheaded weasel was trying to accost her.

Suddenly they were quite literally face-to-face. Their first eye contact from across the room had already left her feeling light-headed enough, but *this* close. . . she didn't know what to do with this close.

Relax, she told herself. *Relax. Be cool. And for God's sake, be nice. No more ass-kicking jokes.*

"You wanted me to kick his ass?" he asked, staring at her intently. "I just thought it would be better to—"

"No, don't even answer the ass-kicking question." She laughed, waving her arms at him. She'd be damned if she couldn't keep her attitude in check. "We didn't need to kick his ass just yet," she assured him, reaching out to touch his shoulder. She stopped her hand just short of actually touching him and pulled it back down to her side, though she wasn't quite sure why.

No, that wasn't true. She knew exactly why. She didn't want to touch him because he was too good-looking.

There were certain men that just looked. . . well, for lack of a better term. . . untouchable. And he was most definitely one of them. Of course, it wasn't the obvious things. It wasn't his chiseled features, or his ocean blue eyes, or the way his coat lay on his slim but muscular shoulders. No, it was all the adorably *imperfect* things that made him so perfect. The way his hair had been cut too short, like he was headed off to summer camp, or the way his tie had been tied just a little too tightly and his shave was just a little too clean and close. He gave a whole new meaning to the term "boyish charm."

"Oh, I'm. . . I'm sorry," he said most politely, pointing his finger back toward the door. "Did you want to kick his ass?"

A wide grin broke out across her face. She wasn't sure if he was being serious or if he was messing with her. And she liked that. If he was just giving her attitude back, that was an extremely good sign, and if he was being completely sincere and actually apologizing for his rudeness in interfering with her potential kicking of ass, well, then that would just be downright adorable. Either way, this was turning into an awfully good day. Her absolute best day in the States so far, hands down.

"Oh, no," she assured him. "Besides," she went on, trying not to fixate on the near supernatural color of his eyes, "it was much more entertaining watching you do your whole. . . book. . . *thing*."

"My book *thing?*" he asked with extreme indignation.

Oh, Katia. The teasing. Watch the teasing.

"My book *thing?*" he repeated emphatically. "That was no *thing*. That was a high-quality kiss-off I pulled off there; that was. . . that was *masterful*."

Katia searched deeper in his eyes, terrified that she'd already managed to alienate the man she'd decided was her favorite person on both hemispheres.

Until suddenly. . . a sheepish grin began to surface on his lips. "Okay, maybe I was overdoing it a little," he admitted as his grin began to widen.

His smile became instantly contagious, and she let out a loud, spontaneous laugh of relief. *Yes.* At least *one* less involuntary alienation in her life.

As her laugh trailed off, she found herself cocking

her head slightly to the side and just studying him. . . .

She still did not really understand him. She didn't even understand how his pretend fumbling for a history book had somehow sent the redheaded weasel on his way. But it was awfully enjoyable to watch nonetheless.

Suddenly they seemed to have fallen into some kind of mutual trance state. She was still determined, however, to at least gather enough breath to obtain his name. "I know you are a history major," she began finally, taking the circuitous route to his name. "You *are* a history major, right?"

"Yes," he confirmed, nodding, and then falling back into their trance for some undeterminable period of time. "Yes."

Okay, the problem was, if he was going to continue to look at her like that, it was going to become very difficult for her to function with even a modicum of normalcy. *Relax, Katia. They are just eyes. Just very blue eyes. Just look into the very blue eyes and talk.*

She looked into the eyes. And he smiled at her. A wide, devastating smile.

Okay, that's not going to work. Look at something else. That's what you need to do. Just look at something else.

She forced her head to turn slightly, finally breaking away from his glance. *Name. All you are trying to get here is his name. Okay, I have an idea.*

"What's your name?" she asked him. *Good. Well done.* She felt for a moment like they were toddlers who'd just met in a playground. No, even a toddler probably could have found a more clever way to ask his name. But still, it had served its purpose.

"Tom," he replied.

"Tom?" she repeated, looking back into his eyes. *Tom.* Now the eyes had a name. "Tom. . . That's the most American name I've ever heard. Tom."

A long, intense pause.

"Well. . . there's 'John,'" he said finally, eyes still unmoving. "John is a more American name."

Now, they could have been talking about anything. They could have been talking about farm equipment, and it would have been just as arrestingly intense.

"Yes, right. . . there's John," she agreed slowly, not sure what she had just said, nor how much time passed after she said it.

"And I'm assuming you have a—"

"Katia," she interrupted.

"*Katia.* . ." His eyes seemed to turn a shade brighter. "*Very* Russian. That's a very Russian name."

Another long, luxurious moment flew by.

"Katia. . ." he began finally, somehow increasing the intensity of his gaze even further. "I just want you to know. . . that in spite of this conversation we're now having, I am not an idiot. I'm actually extremely bright."

"So am I," Katia interrupted, nodding. "I am a

journalist. Well. . . actually, now I don't know if I am a journalist. Now I think I am a singer, but—"

"You're a singer?" Tom asked. On hearing this fact, he seemed to fall back into the intense gaze they were working so hard now to overcome. "You're a *singer*. That's just. . . Can you sing something?"

"Well, if you really want to hear me sing, you should come to my show. Tomorrow night."

"Your *show*." Tom grinned. "You're doing a *show*. Well, *yes*. I mean. . . yes. I'd love to come to your show."

"Or you could also come next week. I do a show every Tuesday night," she said, handing him a flyer with her seductively nonseductive face on it.

"Um, tomorrow sounds perfect," Tom answered, studying her grainy black-and-white likeness, and wondering what painful back story was lurking behind her powerful and brilliant eyes.

Katia took a deep breath and smiled. "Tomorrow night," she agreed.

"Tomorrow night. That's. . . when I'll see you."

He smiled one last time, turned around somewhat clumsily, dropped down the cash for his book at the register, and walked out through that same door she'd seen him come through only ten or fifteen minutes ago. But back then he had only been the most beautiful man in New York City. Now he was Tom. Tom, who was coming to her show tomorrow night.

KENT: Hold on, Tom. I'd like you to stop there. So, then, you didn't go to that bookstore by accident?

MOORE: That's correct.

KENT: One of our agents sent you there?

MOORE: That's correct. Agent Rodriguez sent me there. George was actually with me earlier that afternoon.

NIVEN: That recruitment meeting. . .

MOORE: Yes. Just before I went to the bookstore, George and I were at one of the CIA recruitment lectures at Columbia. I was way too eager to join the Agency, and I'd asked him to come with me and put in a good word. Rodriguez was the agent giving the lecture. That was the first day I'd ever heard that horrible name. . . Nikolai.

KENT: Well, then I think you should go back a little further, Tom. Can you describe more specifically the events just *before* you went to the bookstore—your initial meeting with Agent Rodriguez? Apparently that is when this really all began.

MOORE: That's true. That is when it all started. The picture of Nikolai. . . I'm sorry, John, I should have started there in the first place. Let me go back. . .

He caught a glimpse of *something*. A photo. It passed through the huddle at quite a rapid speed, but **1983** through Tom's eyes, rapid speeds could be reduced to slow motion.

"WELL, THEN I THANK YOU FOR TAKING
the time to come here," Agent
Rodriguez said, "and remember,
your invitations today were
strictly confidential, as was everything discussed in this room. I
know I can count on you for your
absolute discretion. Best of luck to
all of you. I'll be here a few more
minutes if anyone wants to come
up with questions. Thanks."

A Tad Over-ambitious

Tom and George Niven were the only people in the
Columbia University lecture hall clapping as the lights
came back on. There was something a little sad about
that. But then again, popularity and notoriety were
not exactly the CIA's primary goals.

The moment Rodriguez turned his back, Tom
grabbed George by the arm and dragged him toward the
podium. He'd basically forced George to join him at this
lecture. George was, after all, an eight-year veteran of the
Agency. And not only had he been a top-notch com-
mander to Tom in the Green Berets, but he had also
become a top-notch friend after Tom had completed his
service. It was actually still a little strange to see George
in civilian clothing instead of military fatigues, but Tom
was getting used to it. Besides, right now. . . he really
couldn't have cared less what George was wearing.
All he cared about was a personal introduction to

Agent Rodriguez and a very blatant recommendation.

"*Tom.*" George laughed quietly, forcing Tom to slow down as they approached Rodriguez. "*Relax.* I told you I've already put in a good word for you with Rod."

"That's not the same thing as a personal introduction," Tom uttered quietly through the clenched teeth of his strongest smile.

"Has it occurred to you that there might be such a thing as *too* ambitious?" George smiled, pinching Tom's cheek as he sometimes did, knowing how much it infuriated Tom.

Tom knew he was a tad overambitious these days, but it had really only been since Oliver had jumped ahead of him on the Agency track. It had all really come down to that one paper on U.S. policy in Latin America that Oliver had written his junior year at Columbia. Somehow it had fallen into the hands of the intelligence community, and someone up there was so damn impressed, they offered Oliver a job, entry level. But now, here it was only a year and a half later and Oliver was already heading up their code-breaking division while Tom had really done nothing but spin his wheels in the Green Berets and grad school.

Tom and George reached the podium, and George gave Rodriguez a hard slap on the back. "Rod," he said, pulling Tom up next to him.

"Niven," Rodriguez replied with a smile, giving George a firm handshake. But his smile was immediately replaced by a rather wide-eyed reaction to Tom. "My God," he said, with a bemused smile. "The resemblance really is uncanny, isn't it?"

Tom laughed slightly and shrugged. That was all he'd ever learned to do when people had that reaction to him and Oliver, which they always did.

"So *you* must be 'the brother,'" Rodriguez said, giving Tom a firm handshake.

Tom cringed a bit. *The brother? I'm not "the brother"— I'm Tom.* But the smile remained on his face. This was too important a meeting to blow.

"I am," Tom replied. "Tom. . . the brother." *Now smile.*

"Well, I've heard a lot about you, Tom. Your brother can't say enough good things about you."

Thank you, Olly.

"Well. I've heard a lot about you, too, sir," Tom replied. "From Oliver, I mean."

"Tom was my best soldier in the Green Berets, hands down," George added.

"Is that right?" Rodriguez replied, giving Tom's painstakingly trained physique the once-over. "Are you as skilled in the martial arts as your brother?"

Oh, *man.* That was the one question Tom didn't want to hear. But of course he had his patented answer for that one, too. "Well, sir, I'm good. . . but I'm not *that* good." It was an honest answer. Tom had never been able to beat Oliver hand to hand, and he was quite sure he never would be. Oliver was just too good.

Rodriguez smiled back, though his smile had just begun to border on condescending. *Come on, Tom. Stay in this.*

But then, quite suddenly, Rodriguez's smile disappeared altogether. Two well-dressed agents with earpieces and an enviable air of efficiency had leaned in out of nowhere and whispered a barely audible message into Rodriguez's ear. Something was wrong, Tom could tell, and he was dying to know what it was.

"Excuse me one second, Tom," Rodriguez said, turning his back to Tom and huddling with his fellow agents. Tom looked over at George and shrugged slightly. This meeting wasn't going at all the way Tom had hoped it would. George just rolled his eyes, suggesting with subtly outstretched hands that everything was just fine.

"KGB. . ." Tom heard quite clearly amidst their little whispered huddle. He was intrigued. If there was trouble, he wanted to help. If they would just let him in the door, let him inside the world of exclusive huddles and private strategy sessions, he *knew* he could help. If he could just know what was going on. . .

Tom found himself using some of his more advanced visual and auditory techniques to basically peek in on their very serious powwow. It was one thing to have the ability to observe civilians on the street. But to gather intelligence *from* the actual intelligence community. . . well, that was really the name of the game. And Tom wanted to play.

He caught a glimpse of *something*. A photo. It passed through the huddle at quite a rapid speed, but through Tom's eyes, rapid speeds could be reduced to slow motion. He caught red hair. He caught a tweed jacket. And he was pretty sure he'd caught a name: Nicholas or Nikolai. But that was all he would get. The huddle broke up just as quickly as it had started, and Agent Rodriguez replaced that concerned look with an everything-is-fine smile.

"Everything. . . okay?" Tom asked, hoping Rodriguez might trust him with some of the details.

"Oh, everything's just fine, Tom," he assured him, patting him on the shoulder. There was *nothing* more condescending than a pat on the shoulder. "So you're a student, are you, Tom?"

No, not the student conversation. I want to know what's wrong. I want to help. "Yes, sir," he replied with a smile because he had no other choice. "Columbia grad. Trying to complete my thesis in history and historiography." *Can we not talk about it, please? I'd like to know what's happening with Nikolai. . . . Is he KGB? Is he on the loose right now? Does he pose a clear and present danger. . . ? Steer the conversation, Tom. You have to steer it yourself.* "But I'm getting a bit. . . frustrated here in school," Tom added. "I'm really very eager to join my brother in the—"

"You look like a smart kid, Tom," Rodriguez interrupted him. *Kid? A smart kid? Oh, Jesus. . .* "A great education is the key to a successful life, that's for sure."

"Oh, yes, I agree," Tom said, slowly dying inside.

"Historiography, huh?"

"Mm-hm." Tom smiled politely.

"Well, I might be able to help you there, Tom. Tell me, do you have the Latimore translation of *The History of the Peloponnesian War*?"

Books. Now they were talking about books. Agent Rodriguez didn't seem to understand that there were plenty of people here at Columbia with whom Tom could discuss *books*. The last thing Tom wanted to talk about right now was Thucydides.

"No, I can't say I do," Tom replied.

"Well, it's a must for you, Tom. An *absolute must*. I even know where you can pick up a copy in the city. One second."

Agent Rodriguez snapped back to his two silent colleagues for a moment as he pulled out one of his business cards and jotted something down on the back. Then he quickly turned to Tom. "There you go," he said, handing Tom the card. "They'll have the book for sure."

Oh, whoop-de-do, Tom wanted to say. *Another book for my thesis. I sure am glad I dragged George all the way up here and got the haircut and the shave and the new tie. Because this little meeting has just paid off like gangbusters.*

"I want you to go down to that store, Tom,"

Rodriguez said. "I want you to go down there *now*, you understand me? Don't waste another minute of your education."

"Right," Tom replied, trying to keep his posture as straight as possible.

"It was great to meet you, Tom," he said finally, giving Tom another firm handshake.

"You too," Tom replied.

"Now, you go down there right now, and you get that book."

"I sure will," Tom replied. And he wasn't just humoring him. If Agent Rodriguez told him to get some book, that's what he was going to do. If only for the sole reason that it would be something Tom might have to discuss with him if they ever met again.

"Get going!" Rodriguez called out one last time.

"Right," Tom replied in a slight monotone, barely even masking his disappointment at this point. "I'm on my way."

It was as if
she'd been
roaming the
desert for years,
parched and
starving, **2002**
and she'd just
happened upon
this
resplendent
feast.

GAIA COULD SEE THE END OF THE

transcript coming; she just didn't want to believe it. *There has to be something on the last page,* she promised herself, feeling that anxious sense of deprivation that always came with the last few pages of a favorite book. Only this wasn't a

One and One

book she was reliving. These were her parents' lives—their beautiful, romantic lives, lived out just as Gaia had imagined them. . . give or take some staggering resemblances to Gaia herself and a certain heretofore unmentioned KGB agent. But running out of pages. . . that was like losing them all over again.

There has to be some kind of clue or hint or something. . . . She couldn't bear to see all of this exquisite history come to an end. It was as if she'd been roaming the desert for years, parched and starving, and she'd just happened upon this resplendent feast. Biting into these deliciously uncensored chunks of her past was just beginning to bring her back to life. This couldn't possibly be all there was to eat.

But as she flipped over the last page of the transcript, there was nothing more to read. No hints or clues, no *to be continued* written in bold letters, nothing. A moment more and all she could hear over the headphones was air. And then the disc stopped altogether.

She stared at the back of the blue binder for

another sixty seconds in denial, but eventually she had to face facts. That was it. That was all she had. No more journal pages to savor and no more transcript, either. It seemed all the mystery agent had left her with was the most frustrating brand of confusion.

Please don't let this be some kind of KGB scam, she prayed. She dug her hand all around the inside of the manila envelope, but there was nothing. She shoved her hand behind the books in every shelf, making a bit of a mess, but still nothing. She hated this part. The game part was what she didn't have time for. But he'd set the rules in stone, and there wasn't a damn thing she could do about it.

All right, think. Where do you go next? But a moment later Gaia realized. . . the question wasn't where she would go next. The question would always be, where were *they* going next? *Of course.*

She picked up Nikolai's note again and remembered that her mother had written the address of her show on the title page of her father's book. And *sure enough!* That illegible scribble Gaia had seen at the bottom of his note. It wasn't a scribble it all. It had just been written quickly, and it had been upside down on the page:

The Bitter End, 8:30. — Katia

Gaia crammed everything she had into her knapsack and took off out of the Waverly Bookshop at maximum speed. That little trip down memory lane was over, and hopefully the next one was about to begin. She knew where she was headed next. And it was actually only a few blocks away.

Memo

From: KS
To: L

    Security breach confirmed. Several security level 1 dossiers missing from HQ. Missing entire files for subject, Enigma, Loki, and civilian file 48-DG Katia Moore. N has gone missing and has not filed reports for forty hours. Attempts at correspondence have yielded no results. Please advise.

Memo

From: L
To: KS

    Issue APB on N to all affiliates. Initiate immediate and widespread search-and-destroy operation. We must regain those files ASAP. Permission to terminate at will. Report immediately on location of subject.

Memo

From: KS
To: L

    Subject has been spotted on Bleecker Street, west of La Guardia. Entering the Bitter End nightclub.

Gaia's heart
jumped as she
knelt down,
practically
placing herself
nose to nose **2002**
with her
mother, who was
suddenly only
two years older
than she.

THE DOOR TO THE BITTER END WAS

Tragic Groupies

wide open, propped with a crushed beer can to stay that way. They'd probably been using the same beer can to prop that door open since the late seventies. This club had seen everything. Full-fledged folkies in the seventies, new wave freaks in the eighties, and all the imitations of folkies and new wave groups in the nineties.

There was already a band setting up for a show tonight. Maybe even more than one. People seemed to be hustling in and out of the black-walled club nonstop, dragging in their amps and their guitars and various pieces of drum equipment. The place was crawling with dudes in black sleeveless T-shirts and dyed black hair who, if you looked a little more closely, were just way too old to be wearing black sleeveless T-shirts and dying their hair black. Not to mention their chicks, who were all just way too young to realize that their boyfriends were way too old for them.

But this was perfect. Gaia could blend right in with the tragic groupies and no one would ask her a damn thing.

She simply had no idea what to look for. His next clue could be anywhere in the place. It could be backstage, for all she knew. Or it could even not be here at all. The Bitter End was still just a guess on Gaia's part, and given her complete absence of patience at this point, she couldn't predict what she might do if a clue didn't present itself pretty damn quick.

One of the band dudes stopped in front of her, right inside the door, and tacked up a flyer for his band's upcoming show on the large bulletin board. There were so many of those flyers on the board that anyone advertising for their show would only be covering up an advertisement for someone else's show. Gaia stared at the gigantic collage of flyers on the board, every one of them trying to outdo the other with its cyber fonts and its super-annoying band names and its in-your-face imagery. In fact, as Gaia scanned across all the flyers, she realized that there was really only one flyer that seemed at all genuine to her—subdued and *actually* cool in its simplicity. It was just a stark black-and-white picture of a woman's face, with the time and place for the show in the lower corner.

Wait a minute. That's her. That's my mother. . . just. . . younger.

Gaia's heart jumped as she knelt down, practically placing herself nose to nose with her mother, who was suddenly only two years older than she. Which was, just as her father had said, a whole other level of beauty.

Gaia glimpsed the few words in the corner. *Katia, February 16th, 8:30 P.M.*

Yes. This was it. Here amidst all these modern flyers

was this amazing photo relic from 1983, a copy of the very flyer her father had ripped from the brick wall that day—if not the actual flyer itself, given the kind of stuff Nikolai seemed to have access to. Gaia stared at the photo in awe for quite some time. Her father had been absolutely right about the eyes, too. Hypnotic. But once again, the goal here was not just to indulge. This flyer was a clue.

Gaia grabbed the flyer and soon realized joyfully that it was in fact attached to another manila envelope tacked behind the overloaded collage of hopefuls. She tore open the envelope (it was all she could do not to rip it open with her teeth) and pulled out the contents. She had certainly had no desire to go on some kind of treasure hunt, but she couldn't help feeling that the items in her hands were in fact treasures. More journal pages, another binder full of her father's CIA transcript with a minidisc, and. . .

Now Nikolai had added something new. It looked like another transcript of some kind, but the binding wasn't that official blue color of the CIA binder. This transcript was black, and it had another minidisc that clearly accompanied it. The title on this transcript and disc:

Oliver Moore Incident Report—10/16/1990
ORG File # POCC-95547
Digital Transfer

A transcript, yes. From the exact same date as the other one. But *not* a CIA transcript. So what, then? Who had her uncle Oliver worked for in 1990? Had he quit the Agency by then? And how the hell had Nikolai gotten this transcript? Why did she even bother asking that? When Nikolai had said in his note that he had pretty much everything, he meant that he actually *did* have just about everything.

Gaia stepped over to a small table in a dark corner of the room, where she was virtually invisible to all the bands and groupies traipsing through. She pulled the disc player out of her bag, shoved the new Oliver Moore disc in, and pressed play, waiting to hear voices as she examined the rather forbidding black transcript. She saw her uncle's name and then. . . *Nikolai's* name. Very weird. And then someone named Yuri. Jesus. This was getting weirder by the second. And the more confusing it became, the hungrier she was to understand it all. Finally she could hear their voices. The first voice she heard had a deep timbre and a thick Russian accent.

YURI: So. . . [*Pause*] I am waiting. Is there an explanation here? Does *someone* want to tell me what the hell went wrong today?

MOORE: Ask *him.* This was his fault. Don't you blame me for this.

NIKOLAI: This is not my fault. She took me by complete surprise. We were not given proper warning of her capabilities. That is not my fault.

YURI: Is this answer supposed to satisfy me? Moore? Do you think I should be satisfied right now?

MOORE: No, sir, but—

YURI: Don't give me any more goddamn excuses! This is horrible planning, miserable preparation, and a pathetic debacle, a totally unsatisfactory result. So you tell me, Moore. What did we miss here? What factor have you not considered?

61

MOORE: I've already told you, I'm not taking responsibility for this.

YURI: Oh, you are taking responsibility, Moore. Believe me, you are. And we are going to stay here until we have figured out where we went wrong. We are going to go through every detail, Moore, for as long as it takes, until we find what we have missed.

MOORE: Fine. Where do you want me to begin?

YURI: Where do *you* think? At the *beginning,* Moore. I want you to begin at the beginning.

MOORE: What does that mean, sir?

YURI: That means the first day, Moore. The first day you met Katia. You start there, and you tell me what I need to know. Unless you're too much of a fool to remember that far back, which could be part of the problem we seem to be—

MOORE: Oh, I remember. . . I remember everything about that day. Every detail. It was after all, the day I met her. . . .

Just *Katia*.
No last
name. Well,
of course. A
girl this
exquisite 1983
didn't
really
need a
last name,
did she?

OLIVER COULDN'T REMEMBER EVER

having been this tired. Somewhere between six and seven, his
exhaustion had simply gone crit-
ical. And his eyes. . . his eyes hurt
like hell. It was so bad that he
could barely see his own hand
holding the key to his brother's
apartment and fumbling it toward
the lock. He squinted painfully in
the hallway's dim light, trying to
concentrate on opening the door.

Twin Child Prodigies

"Tommy?" Oliver yelled out, getting the door
open. "Tom?" There was no answer.

Oliver flicked on the light, wincing at the glare. He
had done it again—worked so long and so steadily
without stopping that he could barely see straight. The
code was rushing through his head, as it always did
after a day like this, numbers and letters flowing back
and forth across his vision like flocks of restless birds.

"Tommy?" he called out again for good measure,
but nobody was home. Oliver pocketed his set of keys
and made his way to his brother's living room, turning
on a shaded lamp and collapsing onto the couch.

The room was, of course, an absolute mess. It was
always the same way. On long car trips his side of the
backseat had always been strewn with wax paper cups
and Big Mac wrappers from their last stop at the drive

through. Oliver's side was, of course, immaculate. Now, looking around at Tom's apartment, Oliver could see nothing but pizza boxes, papers, magazines—so much stuff that he never even tried to make sense of it when he stopped by.

Sighing, rubbing his closed eyes, Oliver basked in the blessed silence. As much as he wanted to see his brother, see that confident, rakish look on the face that was a near duplicate of his own, he was happy to be by himself for a moment, alone in the dark.

Actually, that wasn't all he wanted, Oliver realized. He wanted a drink. And given that he really didn't drink, he was quite sure he must need it very badly. But that meant getting up off the couch.

If I don't get up now, I never will. He was within a few breaths of dozing off, but he knew what that would mean—he would just dream about the code. He was sure Tom kept a bottle of scotch in the house for all those wild Columbia parties Oliver avoided.

The ice clinked as Oliver filled the glass. If Tom had been here, he would have bothered him about the ice. *How can you put ice in single-malt scotch?* he would ask in that scolding voice of his, but still smiling. *Because I like it cold,* Oliver would say back. He could almost hear the argument in his head as he padded out of the kitchen in his socks, wandering toward Tom's desk.

I like it cold, and it's my drink, Thomas. Oliver was mouthing the words as if Tom were actually there. So what if he put ice in scotch? So what if it made him "look like a dweeb," or however Tom put it? The cold-burning scotch was soothing him, finally, and getting his mind off that terrible code.

The *code.* All the Agency knew was that they'd intercepted some kind of correspondence from the Organization. But that truly was all they knew. The code was driving him *nuts.* And it was frightening him, too, because the fact was—the fact *was,* he wasn't sure he'd ever get it. No, it was worse than that. *The Agency* wasn't sure he'd ever get it. He could tell. He could see it in the blank expressions on their faces, masking their doubts. He knew what they were thinking: *Oliver has lost his edge.* God, wasn't that always the way it worked. You're everybody's golden child as long as you produce results. The second you start to slip even the slightest bit. . . they all start to lose faith. Was *that* the kind of "loyalty" they were always talking about at the Agency? If so, then Oliver would be sure to go and look up the definition of *loyalty* next time he had the chance.

Sipping more scotch, Oliver pulled a scrap of paper from his jeans pocket. Maybe a drink could help him see more clearly? Maybe he was just grasping at straws. Uncrumpling the paper, he stared again at the maddening series of letters and digits. Nothing. It meant nothing. Who was he kidding? Bright, fluorescent CIA office and black coffee or dark, soothing Upper West

Side apartment with a cool drink, it made no difference. Who was he kidding? He had no clue how to solve that code. *Screw it,* he thought, trying to inject some of Tom's voice into his mind. He crumpled up the scrap of paper and hurled it onto Tom's desk. It landed on a pile of other crumpled paper scraps, near a framed picture of the two of them. It was funny. . . Tom just loved those "fighting" pictures.

Tom had one of their kenpo sparring snapshots framed on top of the desk. There was Oliver, at age sixteen, absolutely kicking Tom's butt—not to mince words. It was the viper—the "slashing viper," more accurately—the kick that Oliver had basically invented for himself, a sweet but deadly combination of kenpo and muay thai. He'd tried at least a thousand times to teach Tom the technique all through high school, but somehow, no matter how many times they went over it, Tom always ended up with his face in the dirt. The picture had captured it to a T: Olly holding his stance after executing the kick perfectly, Tom laughing as he pounded his hand down on the mat with frustration. Leaning forward, staring at the old photo, Oliver smiled. Tommy might have gotten all the girls, but Oliver won all the fights.

Oliver looked for a place to put down his drink, but there was none. He couldn't believe how messy Tom left things—it was ridiculous. He moved the

Thucydides book out of the way—and a piece of paper dropped out of it into his lap. He opened it up. . . and then he stopped breathing.

He had never seen a face like that in his life. It was as simple as that. In real life, or in pictures, or in the movies, or even in dreams, he had never seen anything so beautiful. He could feel his pulse racing as he stared at the black-and-white photograph.

Oliver tended to keep his distance from girls—particularly pretty ones. Girls. . . unlike the martial arts. . . were *not* his forte. That was Tom's department. But somehow this was just different. The feeling he got staring into this girl's eyes was something else—an almost desperate urgency. It was a once-in-a-lifetime thing, he thought firmly, the warm glow of the scotch spreading through his body.

And quite suddenly, as if someone had whispered it in his ear, Oliver knew what he had to do. He had to find this girl now. He had to talk to her now. This was just. . . She was the girl for him, there was no question about it in his mind. Oliver knew the reason he'd never gotten close to other girls. It was because other girls weren't *her*.

Katia, it said in the lower-left-hand corner. Just *Katia*. No last name. Well, of course. A girl this exquisite didn't really need a last name, did she? The ice was melting in what was left of the scotch— ruining it, Tom would say. The glass was wet and slippery, printing a dark ring onto Tom's antique desk. Oliver didn't need a last name to find her. He had something better printed directly under her name. He had the exact time and the exact place he could find her. *Just an hour from now,* he thought, his face burning with the heat of the scotch and his own urgent emotions.

Eight-thirty. At The Bitter End. That was where he would find her.

Suddenly the code, the photographs, how tired he was, how his eyes hurt—none of it mattered. It was like the CIA had gone away to some other planet. And five minutes later, as he pulled Tom's door shut and locked it again, racing to catch the next downtown train, it was only Katia's luminous face he was seeing, floating before his eyes and utterly replacing the endless numbers he was so tired of.

"BUT YOU ACCIDENTALLY SHOWED ME

Powers of Surveillance

the photo," Tom explained. "So I recognized—"

"'Accidentally'?" Agent Rodriguez smirked at him. "That was no accident. A confidential surveillance photo of a KGB agent? And I'm letting some grad student catch a glimpse of it? No, that was deliberate, Tom. I'd have to be the worst CIA agent in the world to make a mistake like that. I was hoping you'd figure that out for yourself."

"I missed it," Tom admitted, feeling every bit the fool he apparently was.

Rodriguez waved a hand dismissively. "That was my intention. I *had* to do it that way," he explained. "Anyone can find something if they're *looking* for it. No, what's important is what you see the rest of the time—you can live or die by the details that surround you when you're not looking for anything. And you lived."

"Lived?" Tom asked. "Was Nikolai that—?"

"Oh, there's no evidence he's that dangerous," Rodriguez assured him. "Who is he? What's he doing in Manhattan? What's his connection to the KGB? Right now we simply don't know."

"I see."

"And that's where you come in," Rodriguez said.

Where I come in? What does he mean, where I come in? Tom knew what that sounded like. But of course, it couldn't be what it sounded like.

"Observation, analysis, combat, decryption. . ." Rodriguez went on. "You've demonstrated exceptional strength in all areas, and it is therefore my privilege to welcome you to the United States Central Intelligence Agency, Thomas Moore. If you agree to the terms of employment, your enrollment as an entry-level agent in training will commence immediately."

He *had* said it. Tom was sure he had heard him say it. *Central Intelligence Agency. . . agent in training.* And no alarm was going off. No static-filled music from his clock radio. No Sunday church bells. Just Rodriguez's hand firmly shaking his own. This was real. This was really happening.

"Thank you," Tom said, trying to look proud and competent when all he actually felt was utterly dumbfounded. "I'm so grateful for—thank you, Agent Rodriguez."

"But there's one small snag," Rodriguez added. He was picking up the Nikolai file, checking his watch as he did so. "A little bit of unfinished business. Your thesis."

Tom felt a sinking feeling. His *thesis?* For one glorious moment it had looked like all that was behind him. The elation faded—but just a bit.

"We don't hire quitters," Rodriguez said. "You've got to finish it. And *as soon as possible,* Tom. Time spent on anything else is time wasted—and the CIA takes a very dim view of wasted time. Start tonight. And don't stop until you're done."

"*Tonight?*" Tom choked. He could barely get that word out of his mouth. *Tonight* had meant only one thing to Tom the entire day. *Tonight* meant when he would see her again. *Tonight* meant replacing that poster back home with the real thing. He couldn't start tonight. That was an absolute impossibility. Tonight was for her—and every other night after that if he had anything to say about it. No. It simply couldn't be—

"*Tonight*, Tom," Rodriguez repeated firmly. "When you receive an order in the Agency, you don't question it. Just a little word of advice." Rodriguez leaned closer and probed Tom's eyes, like he was literally searching to see just exactly how much character Tom possessed. "We're looking for something here, Tom," he explained. "We're looking to see just how quickly and consistently you respond to your directives. Honestly, I shouldn't even be telling you that. It's kind of like giving someone the answers to the test. But I like you, Tom. And I admire your brother, so I'm telling you. This thesis thing. This is a test. And you pass the test by committing to it completely and immediately, not halfway. Am I making myself clear?"

Tom felt thoroughly paralyzed. He was between a million rocks and two million hard places. But he had to at least try to say something. "Yes," he said. "Crystal clear, and thank you for your honesty. But I was just hoping that we could start the test tom—"

"Tom, you don't say 'but' in this scenario. There is no 'but' involved. If you say 'but,' it's like failing the test. And I don't want you to fail the test, Tom. Agents who say 'but'. . . they fail the test. And they don't last very long. . . . *Now* am I making myself clear?"

Tom began to nod in spite of himself.

"Whatever it is tonight," Rodriguez went on,

"however long ago you made the plan, whatever her name is. . . those things don't matter now, you understand? They can matter later. Agents drop those things like rain—they drop them the second they get the call. They have to. Because they've been given their directives. Are you going to follow your directives, Tom? Are you going to pass the test?"

Tom had never had a set of consequences explained to him so clearly and succinctly. And it did at this point seem to go without saying that his answer would by definition *have* to be. . .

"Yes," Tom said, heading for Rodriguez's door.

"Oh, and Tom." Tom held up at the door and turned back. "Remember," he said with a smile. "During this test we'll be watching you—we'll always be watching. . . ."

Tom honestly couldn't tell if he was kidding or not.

It's time to be a soldier again.

It's time to make a painful choice and live with it. I'd almost forgotten what it's like to think that way. But George drilled it into my head from the first day of basic training. He said, "A soldier is a man who makes difficult choices and lives with them."

So now I've got to make the difficult choice of letting go of the greatest thing in my life. . . so I can have the *other* greatest thing in my life. Of course that would have to be the case, wouldn't it? Life never lets you have it all at once.

I wonder how I'll be able to mix the two things in the future— my duty as an agent and my duty to the people I love. I'm sure I'll get the hang of it eventually. If people just have some patience. . .

That's the life of the soldier and the spy—impossible choices with outcomes that are too grandiose to consider. But God, I hope Katia has the patience—I really do. Because if I turn away from the job, I'll never be able to call myself a soldier again. And then I would not be able to live with myself. And I'd be absolutely no good to her.

But I *will* see her again.

Please wait for me just a little while, Katia. Please have a little patience. Because I'm coming back to you. Soon. As soon as it can possibly be.

I promise.

PICTURES CAN LIE, OLIVER THOUGHT.

He was seated at a table near the front of the Bitter End, trying to stay calm. He stared at the stage in total, **Irrefutable** avid expectation. If a grenade had gone off at the other end of the room, he probably wouldn't have noticed.

It was eight-forty, and Oliver kept looking at his watch, reminding himself that performances always followed some strange rule that dictated they couldn't start on time. His entire brain was consumed with the photograph of Katia. He didn't even need to physically see it before him—it was burned into his memory, like an old-fashioned iron brand burned into the flank of a bull.

But pictures can most definitely lie, Oliver was thinking. And it was a fact—anyone who'd ever seen a rotten snapshot of themselves or a flattering magazine cover showing a celebrity looking better than humanly possible. . . anyone who'd seen any photo, really, knew that they couldn't always be trusted. Oliver kept telling himself that as he drank the club soda he'd ordered to keep himself from becoming any more intoxicated and stared at the empty stage. He wanted to prepare himself for disappointment. Because there was just no way Katia could live up to her picture.

The long black piano stood onstage, gleaming in the spotlights, in front of the glittering curtain. Oliver tried to keep calm, knowing that she was about to appear. She was going to be right there, just a few feet away—he almost regretted sitting so close.

And then she was there. Simply there. Almost as if by magic.

Oliver remembered reading poems about beauty in school. Like Byron's lines, "She walks in beauty, like the night / Of cloudless climes and starry skies." He realized he had never understood what they really meant. He had thought he did—until tonight.

Katia stepped out onto the small stage, wearing a white cotton dress that seemed somehow to both cling to her body and flow from it at the same time. And as she hovered closer and closer to him. . . well. . . who was he kidding? She was stunning. If anything, her picture hadn't done her enough justice.

"This is a new song," she announced simply as she squinted momentarily to try and see out into the audience. *Russian*. She had the most enchanting Russian accent.

And the moment she began to sing her first song. . . Oliver decided that he'd been wrong all his life about love. Wrong to think he could live without it. He was discovering it now for the first time, and it felt as crucial as oxygen—as the water you gulped down when you found your way out of the desert.

Oliver had always been more partial to classical music. But from her first note on, he knew he was now partial to both classical music and Katia's music. The lyrics to her first song were strange and smart and instantly intriguing, even though he couldn't really make any sense of them.

> Alien Boy Wonder
> I think you've cut your hair too short
> And you've tied your tie too tightly, too
> I think I could share my history with you. . . .

All of her songs were like nothing Oliver had ever heard—filled with so many strange and wondrous dichotomies. Sometimes the melodies seemed so gentle, almost like children's songs, but the words were so hard and bold, like she'd been through so much more than her innocent face and voice suggested. And then sometimes it seemed as if she were simply channeling some sweet melody that had been heaven-sent—her rich and supple voice coasting effortlessly through soaring peaks and gravelly valleys. An angelic voice with such a nakedly earthen soul. The voice cut straight through to the center of his chest and then melted slowly through the rest of him.

He froze in generally the same position of awe for the next half hour.

When he felt her set coming to an end, one thought overtook him. A thought that both thrilled and terrified him: He was going to talk to her. A lifetime of chickening out was finally going to end. Tonight. And what better time? After all of those girls he was too shy to talk to, all those dances where he'd roamed the perimeter. . . he was finally ready.

He would just stand up and walk over to her and say hello, even if it killed him.

He was a loner no more. *Alien Boy Wonder.* . . He had no idea what exactly that meant, but somehow he knew that it was someone he wanted to be.

Three-Legged Puppy

AS A RULE, KATIA TRIED TO FORGET the audience while singing, and focus on the song. But tonight was different. Tonight she was thinking about Tom. His face had been permanently installed in her imagination, floating in front of everything she looked at, like a slide projected directly into her eyes. *He's out there,* she told herself, her voice nearly faltering at the thought. *No, he's not,* she reprimanded herself. *He's not coming. He's already forgotten.*

That was what she was worried about while she sang about love. About him. She was worried about whether she'd imagined it all. Not imagined Tom—he was quite real—but imagined the spark between them. It could happen. You just never knew when you met a stranger. *Especially an* American *stranger,* she told herself over and over. *They can all be so friendly. It's difficult to tell what they're really thinking.*

Katia snuck a glance to her right, into the dazzling spotlights, during the last song. The suspense was killing her. Was he there or not? If he wasn't, she'd have to immediately begin the task of forgetting him. Just to protect herself. You couldn't fall for someone that hard, that quickly, and then *wonder* about it for too long. You had to get out while you still could. It was simple self-preservation.

But if he *was* there— Katia felt her throat trembling as she sang. If he *was* there, it was a whole different story. It meant, simply, that everything she'd felt in the bookstore was real. That thought made her so happy, she deliberately shoved it to one side.

Almost done. The last eight bars—Katia sang as well as she could because if he was there, she wanted him to hear her voice at its best. She actually managed to put all thoughts of Tom out of her head for long enough to finish the song, stand up (without catching the dress on the piano bench, a mistake she'd made at least once), and smile at the audience, bowing graciously.

Bring the lights up, Katia mentally urged the stage manager. *Bring the lights up so I can see him.* Was he there or not? Enough suspense already. It was too exhausting.

There was the familiar *thunk* of the machinery as

the spotlights went out. The house lights (such as they were) came up right then, and Katia stood on the small stage, blinking to clear her eyes, peering out at the collection of candlelit tables that filled the room. . .

And there he was.

Katia stared at his unmistakable, beautiful face. Tom was staring right back at her, as if mesmerized. An incredible rush of relief and excitement coursed through her. She almost lost her footing on the stage, she was so happy to see him. She nearly tripped again, stepping off the stage in her high heels.

Tom was standing up awkwardly, with that same shambling style she remembered. He looked different— he was more carefully groomed. His hair was combed down flat now, and his clothes were pressed. His hair looked *longer*, actually, but that had to be an illusion. It was just the effect of its having been combed.

"Hi," Katia said. Immediately she cursed herself for not coming up with something more clever than that.

"Hello," Tom said, looking back at her. It was strange—she saw none of the adorable rakishness she'd seen in the bookstore. The boyish charm had shifted into something else. . . .

And that was fine. She felt it, too—the gentle slide into a new rapport between them. They couldn't flirt like school kids forever, though she really hadn't minded it so much. It hadn't exactly been under her control. But perhaps this vibe was better. More real.

81

"I'm so glad you came, Tom," Katia said truthfully. She was forcing herself to be much more direct. He was actually *here*—he had come as promised—and he deserved more than just her patented Katia attitude.

"Well. . ." Tom froze for a moment. His eyes suddenly widened, almost as if she'd somehow surprised him with something she'd said. "Of course. . . I'm here, Katia," he replied finally, though quite awkwardly. "I. . . wouldn't have missed this for the world."

"For the world, huh?" She grinned at him, hitting him lightly on the arm. But even that seemed a little strange. Yesterday she hadn't even allowed herself to touch him. He was just as cute as the day before but somehow not untouchably cute. "Pretty high stakes for someone you just met," she added, trying to keep up her end of things.

"Well—nevertheless." Tom grinned that familiar smile, which, as predicted, did still make her somewhat weak in the knees.

Except it *didn't*. That was the funny thing—she couldn't put her finger on it, but the smile had changed somehow. Like the weight of the world had landed on Tom's shoulders. "Is everything okay, Tom? You seem—"

"Everything's just fine, Katia," Tom said. He had come to his senses apparently and was making a sweeping gesture, pulling out a chair for her to sit down. "Won't you join me for a drink?"

"I'd be delighted," Katia said. It was like playing along with a pantomime, like they were total strangers (which, she reminded herself, they practically were). She nodded courteously and accepted the chair he'd pulled out. "So how's the paper going?"

"Paper?" Tom blinked at her so innocently that she swatted him on the arm again. She could do that quite easily now.

"Your *thesis*," she told him with mock frustration. "The one you got the book for yesterday afternoon. I *do* have a reasonably good memory, Tom."

"All right, I'm sorry. Listen, here's the thing—"

Here it comes, Katia thought, depression sinking over her like a heavy blanket. *Here comes the bad news. He's married. He's divorced. He's going to prison. He just got out of prison. He's—*

"I'm not Tom."

Katia wasn't sure she'd heard correctly. "W-what?"

"I'm his brother," the man before her said, his head lowered as if in shame or embarrassment. "His twin brother. My name's Oliver."

"His—you've got to be kidding." Was this another one of Tom's new annoying traits? A practical joker? It wasn't very funny. She looked back into his eyes, considering whether or not to scold him for this ridiculous prank, but. . .

But the thing was, Katia realized, the longer she looked at him. . . those really *weren't* his eyes. She could have forgotten a lot of things, but the eyes? She couldn't have possibly forgotten the eyes. She'd stared straight into them for some infinite amount of time the day before. And these eyes. . . they were the same color, but they were *not* the same eyes. And slowly, dazedly, as she examined his every word and his every feature, the different attitude, the lack of adorable confidence, the generic mannerisms, and particularly the *longer* hair. . . it all made sense. That was why he was having such trouble with their conversation.

It wasn't him. It wasn't Tom.

"What, you're like the evil twin or something?" she said with a laugh. "Trying to play some mind games with me here?"

"No! Nothing like that," Oliver assured her with a laugh of his own. "I didn't even know you two had *met*," he added vehemently. "I just. . . saw your flyer, and. . ." He trailed off and averted his eyes with what seemed like embarrassment again. "I mean. . . how do you know *he's* not the evil twin?" he added with a smile.

Suddenly her heart kind of went out to him for a second, though she had no idea why. There was something a little. . . lost or helpless about him. In a sweet way. And now that she realized he wasn't Tom, he had a sweet smile. It wasn't bad. It was no Tom smile, but it had its own charm. And it was *his*—it was honest. She could see that right away.

"Wait a minute," she said, her back suddenly stiffening up with a new horrible thought. "He didn't send you here in his *place*, did he?"

"*No,*" Oliver assured her. "No, no, no. He would never. . ." Oliver dropped his head in his hands momentarily before turning back up to her with nothing but heartfelt contrition in his eyes. "I'm *so* sorry. I never should have played with you like that. I don't know why I. . . This entire mix-up is entirely my fault."

The more he talked, the guiltier Katia felt for having judged him so harshly. He was right. He was far from an evil twin. He was kind of a sweetheart. In a three-legged puppy dog kind of way.

And now, with a moment to think on it further. . . maybe Tom *was* the evil twin in this scenario.

Evil enough to stand me up, she thought. Although maybe that wasn't fair, either. He hadn't exactly promised he would be here, had he? Katia was confused. Well, how could she not be? The situation had completely changed again—and she still hadn't gotten a drink. Who knew? Maybe Tom was just a pretty face. She wasn't sure of any of it anymore. The Tom-Oliver trick had completely disoriented her.

"Oliver," she said suddenly, "I'm sorry. Let me buy you a drink. Okay?"

"W—what?"

"You don't have to keep paying. And the cover's very expensive here. You know what? Come with me to Chumley's."

"Really?" Oliver smiled in complete surprise and delight, unabashedly, and it was worth it just to see that.

Just to make someone that happy. "Okay—I'd love to."
He sprang to his feet and hurried to get Katia's chair—
something she could *definitely* get used to—and by the
time they were halfway through the crowd, she had
taken the first steps toward putting Tom out of her
mind. He had, after all, apparently had no problem
putting *her* out of *his*. Why should she be any different?

Not that it was easy. . .

She placed her arm in Oliver's and walked to the
door at the front of the club.

But there's that disgusting freak again.

The redheaded weasel, lurking yet *again*, in the
shadows near the door. Leering at her as he always did.

"That man's always staring at me," Katia told him
as they moved for the glowing red exit sign.

"He—he can't be the only—" Oliver stammered. "I
mean, I'm sure you get lots of. . . well, *I* was staring at
you, too," he said finally, blushing madly as he completed the sentence in a near whisper.

"He's different," Katia said, turning her gaze away
from the weasel. "He gives me the creeps."

They hurried out of the club and into the cool
night air. Oliver held both doors for Katia on the way
out, and she did her best to forget about the redheaded weasel. And to forget about Tom.

Was there life before Katia?

I can't remember. I honestly can't—it's almost like it was a gray blur before I met her. She completes me so thoroughly.

Before Katia, I was a different person. I don't think I was fully alive. At least, that's how it feels—how I remember it. It's not that I didn't have things I did every day. I went to school and I had jobs, and I've done well for myself as an agent. I suppose I used to think of that as a full life.

But I was an idiot. That was a *shell* of a life. A crude black-and-white outline of a life. And now I know that, finally. Now I understand what I was missing all those years. I just want to make up for lost time. And this past month has done just that. It has been like ten boring "Oliver years" compacted together into a month of real visceral human experience.

This must be why Tom chased all those girls over the years.

Except, I take that back. This is different from that. It *has* to be. I can't remember everything Tom's said about the girls he's dated—and some of them were quite pretty and seemed interesting, I suppose, each in her own limited way, but I don't know if Tom's *ever* been in love—really in love—the way I am now. Inseparable, I mean. And it is like that for her, too. I can see it in her eyes.

We haven't even kissed yet. That's how slowly we want to take things. That's how much we want to savor all the suspense and glorious tension that comes before that kiss.

But when that kiss comes. . .

It was the
only thing
he'd been
thinking of
all day, even
when he was   **1983**
typing like a
madman: *The
Bitter End,
8:30.—Katia*

OH MY GOD—I'M DONE.

Caffeinated Dance

Tom couldn't believe it.

He couldn't believe he'd made it. It had been nearly impossible to concentrate. Katia's face had floated so maddeningly across his eyes countless times as he'd doggedly poured more coffee for himself and squinted at his typewriter through the long nights. He thumbed through the Thucydides time after time, and every time he had seen her face, the impish smile with which she'd asked him for something to write on. But Agent Rodriguez was right. The Latimore translation of Thucydides had been the missing piece of the puzzle— a puzzle that was now complete.

Tom leaned back in his chair, grinning like a shark as he tossed the final page onto his cluttered rolltop desk. And without another thought, he literally bounced up to his feet with whatever was left of his energy. Because, damn it. . . he had to dance now. He had to. His legs ached in protest, but they could take it.

Finally, when he was quite sure he would either pass out or explode, he gave up his caffeinated dance and gathered the final typewritten sheets, collecting them and shoving them together with the rest of his thesis.

But something caught his eye. There was a page on the desk he didn't recognize. A plain-looking sheet of typing paper that had apparently been crumpled in a ball under all his new stacks of typed-out text. Tom smoothed out the crumpled paper and stared at it with his hyperactive bloodshot eyes. If, after all this madness, he'd handed in a thesis with a missing page. . .

But, he realized, this *wasn't* part of his thesis. In fact, it wasn't even his own writing. The numbered sequences and scribbles were unquestionably his brother's work.

Tom fell back into his chair and stared wide-eyed at the crumpled numbers that Oliver had obviously left behind at some point. And within only a moment or two, staring at the page, his mind buzzing incessantly with caffeine and elation, Tom saw something. He couldn't put his finger on it, but there was something about the numbers—about the sequence—that looked familiar. No, not familiar, exactly, but. . . *organized.* Logical. Like there was a pattern there, a subtle one, but a pattern nonetheless. A *code.* This was a numeric code. And in his bizarre overtired and euphoric state, Tom was quite suddenly seeing through it.

This says something, he realized. *In English.* Grabbing a pencil, Tom scrawled madly on a pad of paper, turning the numbers into letters. It took a little while—maybe forty-five minutes or so; Tom didn't notice time passing at all.

But when he'd finished, he had a string of letters. Most of the letters read like nonsense. But in the middle of two of the lines Tom had found the two very clear English phrases jumping out on the page: *Employ the First Principle,* it said left of center on the third line down. And then, toward the end: *To win her back.*

Win her back? Win *who* back? Tom had no idea what it meant. Still, he thought, leaning back in his chair and rubbing his eyes, not a bad day's work. Was this the "code" that had been driving Oliver so nuts lately? The message they'd intercepted from "the Organization"? Probably not. But Tom let himself feel a moment of genuine pride, anyway. He'd actually done what Oliver, Agent Rodriguez's "resident genius," hadn't managed to do.

But all thoughts of the CIA and codes blew out of Tom's mind the second he glimpsed his watch: 8:00. That gave him only a half hour to get down there. He had finished his thesis just in time. He wouldn't have to wait one more day before he could finally hear her sing, as he'd promised to do so many shameful weeks ago. It was the only thing he'd been thinking of all day, even when he was typing like a madman: *The Bitter End, 8:30.—Katia.*

Semi-telepathic Message

THE FEELING THAT RAN THROUGH TOM'S body was indescribable. Standing near the seedy-looking nightclub entrance, with his hands in his overcoat pockets, the harsh March wind cutting through his too short hair as he squinted up at the black sky and heard Katia's voice for the first time. . . Even ignoring the completed thesis and the broken code, Tom was overjoyed.

He pushed open the door and walked into the club. It was dark, and his eyes took a moment to adjust. A hulking man to one side stopped him, pointing at the sign that indicated the cover charge. Tom fished out a five-dollar bill and handed it over without looking.

And there she was. He was spellbound. The bookstore, four weeks ago, had never really been out of his mind—but seeing her again brought it all back, as if it had happened moments ago.

"*And you've tied your tie too tightly, too,*" Katia sang. "*I think I could share my history with you. . . .*" She was looking at one particular table—the one closest to the stage. A man was sitting there. Tom could see him in silhouette. Of course Katia couldn't actually see that table, Tom realized. The spotlights were shining in her eyes.

Tom moved through the crowd toward the small stage. There was nowhere to sit except that front table with the one man. The closer Tom got to Katia, the harder it was to think clearly, but he knew he couldn't just stand in the front of the club, blocking everyone's view. Hopefully the man would understand.

Tom made it to the front table and gently tapped the man on the shoulder. "Excuse me," he whispered, leaning down. "Do you mind if I. . . ?"

That was when the man at the front table turned—and Tom's body seized momentarily in shock.

"*Oliver?*" Tom whispered.

It was. It was his brother in the flesh. Tom fell into an unusually silent confusion. He could solve all forms of equations and theorems and identities, but seeing the simple mirror image of his brother at this table had left him utterly dumbfounded. And Oliver didn't seem much wiser. In fact, he seemed almost. . . alarmed.

The brothers stared at each other, motionless. Katia's voice had completely disappeared as their eyes locked in the darkness.

"*Tom?*" Oliver whispered, looking sharply at him. He had come to his senses—he was reaching to pull out another chair. "Sit down, sit down."

"Thanks," Tom whispered back, feeling no other real choice at this point but to take the chair. Conversation was out of the question while Katia sang. Tom's ten thousand inquiries would have to wait. Or maybe there was really only one inquiry. That being, *What the hell are you doing here?*

Onstage, Katia was still singing—she hadn't seen or heard a thing.

Offstage, Tom realized that Oliver was staring avidly at Katia.

"*I can wait for you. . .* " Katia sang. Her fingers caressed the ivory keyboard. Her eyes closed as the passion of the song overtook her. Now she was holding the last note, playing the heartbreaking chords that ended the song.

And she was done. The small audience erupted into applause as the lights came back on. Blinking in the sudden brightness, Tom rose to his feet, clapping. Glancing over, he saw Oliver doing the same. A few people in the crowd were staring at them—noticing the identical twins, behaving identically—but they were both used to that.

Katia was coming down off the stage, heading toward their table just as everyone was sitting back down. Her eyes were focused on Oliver—and then suddenly she saw Tom. And she stopped in her tracks.

Now they were face-to-face again. Finally.

And it was like no time had passed at all. She could have been scribbling wildly in that journal just a few seconds ago, and he could have been walking through the door of that cramped dusty bookstore.

"*Tom?*" she said. She was looking at him like she'd seen a mirage.

He knew he should speak, but all he could manage right now was to smile. And smile. And grin. . .

"Well, better late than never," Oliver stated, far too loudly. "Sit down—both of you."

But neither Tom nor Katia paid any attention. Their instant trance state had returned to them, and Tom was in no hurry to let it go. Not this time.

God, I missed you, he wanted to say. But that

wouldn't have done it any justice. That wouldn't have nearly explained the hole in his stomach for the last four weeks. He needed words like *yearning* and *longing* and *craving*. But they all would have sounded so horribly corny—so shamelessly melodramatic. Besides, it didn't really matter what words he would have chosen. He could still barely speak. Nor, did it seem, could she.

"It's not polite to stare," Oliver stated from his seat at the table.

It was an odd statement to make. Bitter somehow. Resentful, even? Whatever its intent, it broke the trance long enough for them to at least dimly notice their surroundings again.

"Did. . . did you finish your thesis?" Katia asked, trying to forge some kind of normal conversation. She was nearly stumbling over the hem of her dress as she moved to the table. Oliver had gotten up to pull out a chair for her, but she almost missed it and toppled to the floor. Tom noticed that Katia didn't even thank Oliver—she kept staring back at him. And that was just fine.

"About an hour ago," Tom said, reaching blindly for his chair and nearly falling into it.

And then their eyes were glued together again. Tom wondered if he might be able to send a semitelepathic message to her across the table—a message suggesting that they leave here now together and find someplace where no sounds could possibly distract them. But a dim thought seeped into Tom's brain.

Oliver. Your brother. Next to you. Whatever his brother was doing here at Katia's show, the fact remained that Tom had barely seen him in the past month, either. And he had missed him.

"Wait—" Tom forced himself to look at Oliver. He reached over and clapped his brother on the arm. "I'm sorry. Oliver! How's it going? What are you *doing* here?"

"Just listening to Katia sing," Oliver said. He was smiling at them both, his eyes moving back and forth. Back and forth. . .

"Yes, I see that," Tom replied. "But how did you know about her—?"

"It's a long story," Oliver interrupted with a trivializing smile. Apparently that conversation was over. For now.

"Congratulations," Katia said, taking another stab at normal conversation. "On your thesis, I mean. Very long sentences, I hope."

"For miles," Tom replied, wanting to take her hand. "God bless the semicolon." And then their eyes locked again. Tom lost track of his thoughts. He had to forcibly remind himself of what he was saying. But Katia saved him by standing up out of her chair.

"You know. . . you boys will have to excuse me for a moment," she announced, patting down her hair and her dress. "But I must, as the American euphemism goes, 'powder my nose.'" She pointed her finger straight into Tom's face. "And *you*. If you disappear again while I'm gone. . . then I will hunt you down and I will—"

"I'll be right here," Tom interrupted. "I promise."

Katia searched his eyes for a moment. "Hm," she grunted, with not exactly mock suspicion. "We'll see. . . ."

Sitting alone with Oliver suddenly made Tom feel very fidgety. For the first time in as long as he could remember, he had no idea what to say to his brother. Oliver had been awfully quick to dismiss his earlier question—the question of just what exactly he was doing at the Bitter End this evening—and now Tom wasn't sure what stance to take. He wasn't angry. Oliver obviously wasn't the type to try and move in on Tom's girl. . . if Tom could even call her his girl. Oliver wasn't the type to move in on anyone's girl. He wasn't even the type to move in on a girl who was one hundred percent unspoken for. No, it wasn't anger Tom was feeling. It was something more along the lines of "suspicious confusion," if there was such a thing. But even that made Tom deeply uncomfortable. He didn't like the idea of there being "suspicious *anything*" with his brother. What he really wanted was to break the tension that was building between them as they sat in silence at the table.

"Oliver," Tom said, squeezing his brother's arm, "I'm in."

"What?" Oliver narrowed his eyes, looking back at Tom. Apparently he, too, was suffering from "suspicious confusion." "What do you mean, 'in'?"

"I mean I'm *in*," Tom said more quietly, leaning closer to his brother. "On Rodriguez's payroll. . ."

Come on, Olly. Don't let one awkward moment ruin something we've been waiting for our whole lives. Whatever is going on here tonight, we'll work it out. This is so much bigger than some misplaced suspicious confusion. This is us. This is Tom and Oliver. . . .

It took Oliver just a second, and then his face lit up with genuine elation. "You son of *bitch*," he whispered joyously. "You *did* it. I'm so proud of you, Tom. I knew you could do it."

All of Tom's suspicious confusion melted away in that moment. This was who they were. Not those silent, fidgety fools who were sitting at the table ten seconds ago, but two brothers who were there for each other no matter what. Two *agents* now. It hardly seemed possible.

"Tell me," Oliver insisted with a grin. "Tell me all about it."

Tom looked over Olly's shoulder and saw Katia gliding back toward the table with her patented angelic grace. She gave Tom a completely unfettered smile. She seemed to be acknowledging that he'd kept his promise this time. He was still there, just as he said he would be. Tom grinned back at her. *Don't worry, Katia,* he wanted to say. *I'm here now. I'm here for good. And I will never make you wait again.*

"Tom?" Oliver was looking curiously into Tom's eyes, still waiting for a response. "Tell me. What happened with Rodriguez?"

"Later," Tom said, his eyes glued once again to hers

as she smiled. "I'll tell you all about it later."

Oliver turned behind him, the proud smile still spread across his face as he followed Tom's enchanted gaze. But when he turned back. . . he was no longer smiling.

OLIVER WAS CONFUSED. SUSPICIOUSLY
confused.

Sitting at their table at the Bitter End, he moved his eyes back and forth, watching his brother and his girl (he secretly thought of her as "his girl") talking, and a feeling was growing inside him—an emotion that was getting louder and louder, like the roar of an approaching train. And it had been a damn near perfect night until Tom showed up.

Putting Sentences Together

"So how was your. . . I mean. . ." Tom was fumbling for words. Oliver watched, a bit smugly. For once it was Tom who was struggling to impress a woman.

"My. . . ?" Katia said, smiling dazzlingly at Tom.

"Your. . . um. . ."

"I'm waiting." Katia kept smiling.

She's leaning forward, Oliver noticed suddenly. It was

true: Katia had curved forward in her chair, her chin on her hand, her face closer to his brother's. He tried to remember if he'd ever seen her sit that way before.

"How was the set?" Tom asked. "There. . . yes," he said with a laugh. "There it is. How was the set?" He was making a show of having completed the sentence successfully. And there was something about it Oliver didn't like. *He's showing off,* Oliver thought. Which was ridiculous—Tom was reacting to a joke. It was the same kind of sly banter Oliver had performed back four weeks ago during that brief, dazzling moment when Katia thought he was Tom. Oliver remembered doing the same kind of thing: the James Dean squint, the casual smile, the hoarse voice, all the little tricks in Tom's arsenal. "I'm sorry I missed it. I really wanted to get here on time."

"That's all right." Katia shook her head dismissively.

"No, really," Tom said. "From what I caught, at the end, that last song was just—"

"You heard the last song?" Katia suddenly looked quite thrown. Bizarrely vulnerable in a way Oliver had never seen before. Why was she suddenly so down on the last song? She'd been closing with that "Alien Boy Wonder" song for the last three shows.

Oliver noticed she was out of wine. "Waiter! Waiter!" he called out as one of the red-vested waiters came by. The waiter didn't see or hear him.

Katia and Tom didn't hear or see him, either, it seemed. And Tom was looking right at Katia's wineglass—her empty wineglass—but he wasn't doing anything about it.

Cad, Oliver thought.

And immediately he regretted the thought. This was probably the best day of Tom's life—he was joining the CIA, and the historiography thesis—the weight hanging around Tom's neck for the last few years—was finally gone. Oliver could see a shaving nick on Tom's cheek and realized he'd gotten ready very quickly. Like he was in a big rush to get down here. And that somehow made the sick feeling grow even worse.

"Waiter!" Oliver called out helplessly. The passing waiter glanced at him, a shadow of irritation passing over his face, and Oliver realized he'd spoken much too loudly.

But not loudly enough to rouse Tom and Katia out of what they were doing—which was, apparently, nothing but staring. At each other. Then, as Oliver watched, Katia actually reached with her slim hand and touched Tom's cheek, where the shaving nick was.

"You hurt yourself," she said, pouting.

"A mere flesh wound," Tom replied, jerking his head so that his face pulled back from her fingers. As if he didn't want to be touched—or touched by her.

As if he didn't want Oliver to see. As if he didn't realize that Oliver had already seen enough.

"Yes, sir?" the waiter said suddenly. He had appeared right next to Oliver, making him jump. Tom and Katia noticed, too—they both looked startled or flustered as they turned their heads to see who had arrived at the table.

"The lady would like more wine," Oliver said weakly. It sounded wrong to his ears—much too formal.

"Thanks, Olly," Tom said, touching Oliver on the arm. "You read my mind. Can I have a Dewars on the rocks?"

"Actually, nothing for me," Katia told the waiter. "I've got to get home."

Oliver was looking at Tom. There shouldn't have been anything irritating about what Tom had done. There was no reason why the casual touch of his brother's hand on his arm—as if he was some kind of servant, on the side, whose job was to wait for the appropriate moment and summon the waiter—there was no reason that should have bothered Oliver. There was no reason it should have made Oliver want to smash Tom in the face. But it did.

"You *really* have to go?" Tom was saying.

"I'm afraid so," Katia said, rising to her feet. She turned to Oliver with a big, friendly smile—but the smile looked forced somehow. "Oliver—thanks so much for dinner. It was wonderful to see you, as always."

"Don't mention it," Oliver said. He could hear the crack in his voice. He stood up, leaning to kiss Katia's cheek. Tom was still seated, accepting his scotch from the waiter. *Stand up, jerk,* Oliver thought angrily. The rudeness bothered him.

"Farewell, ex-historian," Katia said to Tom. She didn't move toward him at all—she just stood there in her flawless white dress, a few strands of hair caught across her face, catching the candlelight like spun copper.

"Bye," Tom said, smiling back at her. He didn't move—he and Katia didn't get anywhere near each other—but as they locked eyes, their faces flushed, their lips slightly pursed, as if they were each about to speak but restraining themselves, Oliver felt the sick sensation grow even more until it seemed to be blackening his vision.

"Oliver?" Tom was leaning forward with a worried look on his face. Oliver wasn't looking—he was staring at the candle flame, watching it dance in the warm air—but he could recognize the concerned voice. "Oliver? Are you all right? What's wrong?"

Oliver looked at Tom. He just looked at him, but Tom recoiled as if he'd seen a ghost—as if his brother's identical face had been replaced by a monster's glaring, bright-eyed stare. Oliver forced himself to smile.

"Nothing's wrong," he told Tom. "Nothing at all."

Banging
loudly on a
door wasn't
exactly a
known
counter-   1983
espionage
maneuver,
but anything
was possible.

SOMEONE WAS POUNDING ON THE

Ghostly Light

front door, and it was getting louder.

Tom reached into the closet and pulled out his service pistol—it was a Ruger .45, loaded clip, empty chamber. He flicked off the safety and approached the front door in his pajama bottoms, gun behind him. He could barely see. Banging loudly on a door wasn't exactly a known counterespionage maneuver, but anything was possible. Leaning so his shadow wasn't visible under the front door, Tom peered through the peephole. And then he instantly relaxed.

It was Oliver. He looked terrible. He was swaying, still dressed in the same clothes he'd worn at the Bitter End, but his hair was a twisted mess. His face was dirty, as if he might have been crying, or throwing up, or both. He smelled terrible. His overcoat and tie were smeared with dirt and mud. His fist was raised, as if to knock on the door again.

"Olly?" Tom said, alarmed. He could tell from his brother's eyes that he was completely drunk. And Oliver *never* drank, Tom reminded himself. There had been a club soda in front of him at the Bitter End. "Olly? What happened?"

Oliver swayed and toppled and would have crashed to the floor if Tom hadn't caught him. Tom's bare feet slipped on the polished floor, his large bare arm muscles straining with his brother's weight. He was overwhelmed with pity and concern. This was a first—he simply had never seen Oliver drunk, in all the years of their adult lives.

"Stole my girl," Oliver was whimpering, his dirty face against Tom's neck. "Stole my girl—you son of a bitch. . ."

Tom suddenly realized that there were small tears flowing sideways from his brother's clenched eyes, drawing clear lines in the soot on his reddened face. Tom brushed his fingers through Oliver's hair, kneeling beside the couch. "It's all right, Olly," he whispered. "It's all right."

"All ri'?" Oliver whimpered. "No, ish *not*—never be all ri'. You son of a bitch—you stole my girl—my *love*—my *Katia*."

Tom looked at Oliver, his eyes widening in surprise.

He loves her, too, Tom realized. He hadn't put much thought into Oliver's presence at Katia's performance—and he should have, he realized now—but it occurred to him for the first time that there might be more going on between Katia and Oliver than he knew. A *lot* more.

This is bad, Tom realized. *This is really bad.*

"Tom," Oliver rasped. His eyes were open; he had stopped crying. He had reached out and grabbed Tom's wrist—even in this state, his grip was strong and unyielding. "Tom, you got—" He cleared his throat painfully; it involved a lot of harsh coughing. "You got to understand. I love her. I can't think about anything else, bro."

"I understand," Tom said helplessly, still brushing Oliver's messy hair away from his face. "I understand."

"I don't think you do," Oliver said, his reddened eyes slipping shut and opening again. "Always got the girl, Tommy—an' now you want this one, too."

"Nothing's happened," Tom said urgently, soothing Oliver. "Listen to me. *Nothing* happened between me and Katia, Olly. That was—tonight was only the second time I ever saw her. I've never touched her. Nothing's happened."

"Going to," Oliver whispered as he looked up at his brother's face. "It's all falling apart, Tom. Nothing's *working*. You've got the girl again. I'm losing the girl... and I'm probably gonna lose the job, too."

"What?" This was the first Tom had heard of anything like that.

Oliver barely curled his hand into a fist as he slammed it clumsily on the back of the couch. "That *code*," he muttered. "Can't even crack that goddamn *code*, Tom. And they *know* it. They can see me losing it... losing the touch... losing everything...."

The *code*. Tom had actually forgotten about it tonight. The code he had proudly cracked only hours ago. Jesus, was Oliver in *that* much trouble with it?

Tom had no idea. But the thought of it adding to his brother's unwatchable drunken sorrow for even another second was simply unacceptable. Here was at least one problem Tom could solve right now.

"That code?" he said with a comforting grin. "Forget about it, Olly. You don't ever have to worry about that code again because I—"

Tom suddenly froze midsentence, like he was slamming down the brakes of a car that was about to go careening off a highway.

What, are you crazy? Tom hollered at himself before he could utter another word. *Have you been listening to your brother at all? He thinks you've stolen his woman away from him, and now you're going to tell him that you cracked a code in forty minutes that's been torturing him for weeks? Do you want him to blow his brains out right here on your couch? Do you want* him *to blow* your *brains out?*

"You *what?*" Oliver asked groggily.

"Huh?" Tom uttered.

"Don't worry about the code because you *what?*"

"Oh. . . nothing," Tom said. "I don't even remember what I was saying." He wouldn't have to tell Oliver about cracking the code. He had a much better idea. But now wasn't the time to think about that. Olly's eyes were finally beginning to close as his breathing became more regular and less labored. And finally, after a few more indecipherable drunken mumblings, Oliver was asleep.

Tom stood up, retrieving the gun off the floor. He pulled off Oliver's shirt and shoes and got a blanket from the closet, draping it over his brother's disheveled form. Tom's heart was heavy as he did it. It wasn't just the pain of seeing Oliver like this. It wasn't just the sudden knowledge that they were in a bad spot.

It's going to get worse, he realized, standing in the dark living room, gazing down on his sleeping brother. *A lot worse.*

But it was something else, too.

I've done this before, Tom thought as he looked down at his brother, looking so pale and almost sickly in his undershirt under the blanket. And it was true. He had done this before. It was completely familiar. . . .

He was the
first one to
say the
word, to
mention
death. And 1973
he was so
sorry to
have
said it.

"WHAT'S WRONG?" TOM CALLED OUT.

"What's wrong with Olly?"

They all looked at him and the doctor looked at his parents, and Tom flinched, expecting them to yell at him, to tell him to go back to bed. But his father had held out a hand, beckoning him, instead.

Antiseptic and Right Guard

"It's all right," his dad told the doctor as Tom ran over and pressed himself against his parents as if he were a little boy again and not a thirteen-year-old kid. "Go on, Doctor. This is Oliver's brother, Thomas. He's old enough to hear this."

The doctor looked down at Tom—up close, he smelled of antiseptic and Right Guard—and then smiled. His glasses flashed as he talked. "Hello, Thomas. Your brother is very sick. He has a rare blood disease called metastatic immune syndrome. And I'm afraid the prognosis is—well, it's not very good."

"Is he going to die?" Tom asked.

He could tell from the way his mother reached out and clutched him, that he was the first one to ask. And he was so sorry to have said it—the adults were being so careful not to. But he had to know. He had to.

"There's no known cure, I'm afraid," the doctor said finally. He spoke very carefully. "I'm sorry,

Thomas. We're going to do everything we can, but the truth is that he probably will not make it."

Tom's mother was crying now—he could feel her hand shaking on his shoulder—and just as his own eyes blurred, he broke away from her and pushed past the doctor with his Right Guard and his glasses and ran into Oliver's room.

Oliver's room was neat as a pin as always, his schoolbooks and board games neatly stacked, but the bed was surrounded by unfamiliar, strange objects now. There was a tube coming out of his nose and boxes of medicines and pills all over the place and a strange machine that made frightening noises as if the machine itself was breathing. There was a horrible smell of medicine that made Tom gag as he came right up to the bed, and he wanted to cry out in shock because Oliver looked so thin and small. He was breathing slowly, his eyes closed, the IV connected to a bruised patch on his frail-looking arm.

Tom couldn't bear to look—but he came closer, brushing Oliver's hair away from his face. Tom realized that he would do anything, anything at all, to make his brother come back. He would let him win at chess, he would give him his *Star Trek* action figures—even Mr. Spock—anything at all.

If he dies, Tom thought, *I'll die, too.*

"I'll save you, Olly," Tom said, wiping his eyes. "I promise."

"Tom, that's enough, dear," his mother's voice came from the corridor. "He's very weak now."

But Oliver's eyes were fluttering a bit—just for a second it seemed like his brother was awake and could see him.

"You just sleep now," Tom whispered, brushing Oliver's hair from his forehead. "I'll take over from here."

My dad had a mainframe—an IBM 1130, I think. Nothing like today—this was before the Internet, before floppy disks, before color screens. The computer system was in Dad's office, and we weren't allowed in there at all. But I snuck in there late that night after Mom and Dad had gone to sleep.

The whole thing made lots of noise, but fortunately Dad had taken that into account when he set up his office, and the walls were soundproofed. The computer itself was the size of an elevator car or a meat locker, and you had to use these stacks of punch cards to program it. But I got the hang of it, actually. I kept thinking about Mr. Spock, on *Star Trek*, and how he could always master a strange alien computer after about ten minutes of examining it. If Spock could do that, I thought, I should be able to handle a measly twentieth-century Earth computer.

Like I said, there was no

Internet in those days, but there were database networks. You could push the phone receiver into this machine with rubber cups, and there would be this faint squealing noise as the computer talked to its cousins—very slowly. My biggest fear those nights was that one of my parents would wake up for some reason and try to use the phone and hear that high-pitched scream of primitive digital communion.

So I looked at the university's database—my father's main modem connection—and began finding ways to explore other databases, too.

It took me five nights to even get in the right ballpark—to find the primitive medical library resources that existed at that time. But finally one night, just as I was about to turn the massive machines off (since the warm machinery would give me away the next morning), I found something.

A clinic. The Institut Pasteur in Paris. It was the only medical center in the world actually doing research on Oliver's disease. And I had *found* it.

My mother and father were angry at first, thinking I'd just been snooping around Dad's office. I remember Dad had started to scold me when Mom suddenly grabbed his sleeve and wordlessly pulled him over to the big green screen, where they could see what I'd found. An actual clinic with an actual treatment. . . albeit an extremely experimental treatment.

But they got excited. Truly, truly excited as they peered at the green words on the screen and scrambled madly for the phone, explaining what I'd found to Oliver's doctors.

My father took a hiatus from work, flew with Olly to Paris, and checked him into the clinic for five weeks. I remember my father's ashen face as he took Mom aside to make the decision. I had read all the reports on his computer—I knew that the risks of the treatment were tremendous—liver and lung damage, possible mental disorders later in life, and even the potential for permanent sterility. But my mother just nodded silently, accepting the risks. Because we all knew it was either take those risks or let him die. And we all hugged. And that was that.

I never *did* tell Olly about all the potential side effects. And I don't think I ever will—I mean, the important thing is that he emerged unscathed. His gratitude was so pure when he was discharged, smiling at me from the infirmary chair—why cloud it?

So I learned about computers, of course, but more important, I learned about *hope*—about never giving up. It's probably the most important lesson I learned as a teenager. It helped me time and time again in the Green Berets and as a grad student. Never give up—there's *always* a way. I'd *proved* it. And I'd never risk losing Oliver again. Never.

Tom was
silhouetted
against the
bright blue
sky, like a
Roman
statue of a
gladiator,
his
musculature
backlit.

WHERE THE HELL AM I? OLIVER thought vaguely, trying to stay asleep and failing. *What time is it? What's that noise?*

The Hangover Gods

And then, with the sound of stumbling footsteps, it all came clear. His brother's apartment. He was on the Upper West Side of Manhattan, in Tom's messy living room, on the sofa. With one beauty of a hangover.

And the phone was ringing. That was the terrible sound that had awakened him. It was like an air-raid siren, and Tom was wincing at it, too. "All *right*," Tom whimpered, and Oliver resisted an urge to smile. Finally Tom had managed to fumble the phone to his ear, stopping the siren in midwail, and the blessed relief of that was almost enough to counteract the terrible expanding pain in Oliver's head.

"Hello," Tom said into the phone. His voice was scratched and fuzzy with sleep. "Tom Moore."

Without moving, Oliver found himself straining to hear the other end of the conversation—but it was no use. His CIA training included listening techniques— he was tuning out the traffic noises from Morningside Drive, out the window, and the sudden hissing steam of the radiator—but he couldn't hear a thing.

"Oh—good *morning*," Tom said. He had shifted

the phone to his other ear. "Is it morning? Just barely."

And that was the funny thing. Oliver could always tell, from Tom's tone of voice, who he was talking to. Not exactly who it was, but whether it was a man or a woman. It was something in Tom's inflections—he couldn't put his finger on it.

But this was clearly a woman.

"Of course I know who this is," Tom said. He was keeping his voice down—he glanced over at Oliver to see if he was still sleeping. *Definitely a woman on the other end of the phone,* Oliver thought. The headache got worse as the details of the previous evening flooded back, and with a sick feeling he realized which woman it was.

"No, no—I was awake," Tom was saying. Oliver had his eyes closed again—he had closed them instantly as Tom had glanced over—but he could tell from Tom's voice that he was grinning.

"No, no, don't worry about *that,*" Tom continued. "That was fine. You were tired—I understand."

Oliver wanted to fall back asleep, now. His dream had been awful, but it was better than this. The headache and the bright sunlight and the queasiness, and the fact that Tom was on the phone with Katia, right in front of him. The more he woke up, it seemed, the worse it felt.

"Well, this isn't"—and again, through his eyelashes, he saw Tom glancing in his direction—"this isn't the best time to talk about—what? Tomorrow night?"

Let me fall back to sleep, Oliver prayed to the hangover gods. *Please.*

But the hangover gods didn't listen. Oliver was too inexperienced to know that they almost never did. The most you got out of the hangover gods was a bottle of water in the fridge—if you were lucky.

"Tomorrow night is fine," Tom said. "Yeah—I'll see you there. Eight o'clock—perfect. Bye." And he hung up.

Oliver tried to remain motionless, but it was impossible. He was too tense.

"I know you're awake, Olly," Tom said.

Oliver opened his eyes, wincing in the glare. Tom was silhouetted against the bright blue sky, like a Roman statue of a gladiator, his musculature backlit. "Morning, Tom," he said hoarsely. "Sorry about last night."

"You never could fool me with that fake sleep routine," Tom said. "Come on—we need showers, and then you can let me buy you some breakfast."

"I heard the conversation, Tom," Oliver said, sitting up. "I know that was Katia. I know what you're doing."

"All right." Tom sat down in his easy chair. "We're both sober, so let's talk."

"Do we have to?"

"No—*listen* to me, Olly." Tom leaned forward, elbows on knees, a terribly earnest expression on his face. "Obviously you and Katia have become—have become friends."

"I don't like this already."

"You've become close. So maybe she told you that we met a month ago, she and I, in the Waverly Bookshop."

"Tom—"

"A *month* ago, Olly. And last night was the first time I'd seen her since then. Honest. I would *never* try to steal a woman away from you. You *know* that, Olly. I would *never* go behind your back."

Oliver was rubbing his eyes, trying to take this in. His left side ached terribly, and he realized he must have fallen onto cement more than once while staggering uptown the previous night. "I know, Tom. I mean, of course I know that. You'd probably swear it on the Bible."

Tom made a Green Beret salute. "On my honor as a soldier, Oliver. I swear. Nothing happened between us since we met. She just called now because, well"—Tom shrugged maddeningly, as if he were saying, *Hey, it's not my fault I'm so damn cute.* "She just called because she called," Tom concluded.

"All right," Oliver said. All he wanted was to get *out* of here—to get away from Tom and his earnest, bare-chested confessional. He rose to his feet, leaning on the edge of the couch to steady himself. "All right, I understand. You don't have to say anything else."

"So everything's cool?"

Oliver forced himself to make eye contact—he stared for one hateful moment into Tom's ice blue eyes before he had to turn away.

"Yeah, everything's fine. Thanks again," Oliver said.

"Where are you going?" Tom said as Oliver got his coat and stumbled toward the door. "Wait—have coffee. Stick around."

"Thanks anyway, bro. I've got to get back downtown. I'm sorry about all this."

"Oh, anytime, Oliver," Tom said expansively. *Now that I've got what I want,* Oliver imagined him thinking. He couldn't get out of the apartment fast enough. "Anytime at all."

The apartment door slammed shut behind Oliver— he winced as the noise slapped his eardrums—and he stumbled down the stairs, thinking crazily that he never wanted to come back to this place again.

For a moment there, he had actually felt more connected to a self-proclaimed **1983** terrorist than he had to his own twin brother.

"TOM!" AGENT RODRIGUEZ SAID. HE

was leaning around the
corner, waving at him.
"Come on in."

Tom bounced to
his feet and followed,
not wanting to look
too eager. He needn't

Alphanumeric Resequence

have bothered: Agent Rodriguez had already continued on. Tom had to sprint to keep up as the agent led
him through a buzzing security door and then around
corners into a small briefing room. Tom took the seat
that Rodriguez had gestured toward.

"First, here's your badge," Rodriguez said, tossing
a leather case across the table. Tom caught it, trying
to seem bored, fingering the leather case. "Go
ahead—take a look," Rodriguez added. He seemed
amused. Tom unsnapped the case and looked at
the CIA badge. He had seen Oliver's, of course—he
knew what they looked like. But now he finally had
his own.

"Thank you," Tom said. He slipped the badge into
his pocket.

"Not at all; congratulations on your thesis." Rodriguez
was looking at his watch. "Was there something else? You
had requested a personal meeting."

"Yes," Tom said, leaning forward nervously. He
had been rehearsing this in his mind since watching

his brother pass out as he complained of losing everything—the girl *and* the job.

The question of Katia wasn't something Tom could help his brother with. He knew that in his heart. But the *job*. Tom was pretty damn sure he could do something about the job. Then at least he would be helping to relieve *some* of Oliver's pressure. And judging from earlier this morning, Oliver very much needed for some of the pressure to be relieved.

"It's about my brother," Tom said. "I know that he's been struggling a bit lately with this one particular code—an intercepted correspondence from the Organization?"

"That's true," Agent Rodriguez said. He was squinting at Tom, and Tom had to take a deep breath and work up the nerve to continue.

"That happens from time to time, you know," Tom went on. "Sometimes even the greatest minds can get blocked on something for no particular reason. It doesn't mean that they've lost their ability; don't you agree?"

Rodriguez looked utterly bewildered and perhaps a little impatient. "I'm assuming there's a point here, Moore." Rodriguez smiled. "And I'm assuming you're going to make it now."

"Yes, sir, there is," Tom said. He dug into his jacket pocket and pulled out a crumpled piece of paper—the paper of Oliver's that he had found on his desk the day before. Tom had taken a red pen and written in the decoding algorithm he'd come up with. "Sir, the thing is. . . that code that's been tripping up my brother, well. . . I think I sort of accidentally solved it last night."

Now Tom had Agent Rodriguez's attention. His eyes widened slightly and his posture straightened as he reached out his hand for the piece of paper Tom was holding. Tom handed the page to Rodriguez, who put on a pair of reading glasses as he peered down at the red writing.

"That's the decryption," Tom explained. "Something about 'the first principle' and 'winning her back,' although I don't understand what—"

"*You* solved it?" Rodriguez asked. He was staring at the page incredulously.

"Yes, well, it was a *total accident,* sir," Tom assured him with a self-deprecating laugh. "Just one of those sort of freaky flukes that comes along every now and then, but. . . what I was hoping, sir, was that now that this particular code has been solved. . . I hoped that maybe you might be able to finally move Oliver on to the next assignment. Something fresh, you know? I know that this particular code really got under his skin and bogged him down, but with a new assignment—a new code, that is— I think you would see the old Oliver back in action. I think freed up of all the stress from that code, he'd be poised and raring to go for the next challenge."

Okay, Tom, relax, you're talking too much.

"Winning her back," Rodriguez murmured, staring at the paper. "Son of a bitch—you're right. An alphanumeric resequence—incredible." He suddenly looked at Tom. His expression was both surprised and pleased. "Good work, Moore. A fantastic job."

"Well, thank you, sir, but really, I don't even know how I solved it. It just hit me all together in one moment. But about Oliver. . . do you think you could move him on now to the next assignment? Let him put this one snag of a code behind him?"

"Well, of course, Moore, of course," Rodriguez replied, deeply engrossed in the encryption. "Why would I keep him on a code that was already broken?"

"*Exactly*," Tom agreed, breathing out a long, relieved exhalation. This was exactly the reason he had come, and now he was very glad he had. He had just successfully made life a little easier for his brother, and he was feeling awfully good about it.

But then a dark bit of nervous energy suddenly chimed into Tom's head. *The conditions,* he reminded himself, *don't forget to tell him the conditions.* "Oh, there is one other thing," Tom said, trying to pull Rodriguez's attention away from the document he'd just handed him. "I'd *really* appreciate it, sir, if we could *not* tell my brother about this meeting—about my solving the code, I mean. Things have been a bit tense between us right now, with me entering the Agency and such, and. . . if it's all right with you, I'd very much like for Oliver never to know who solved this thing. . . . Sir?"

Rodriguez finally shot his head back up for a moment. "Hm?" he grunted, reaching for his phone. "Yes, of course, Moore, of course. No worries. Hello, Lowy? Rodriguez. Is Guinsberg there?. . . Guinsberg? Rodriguez. Listen, I've got the solution." He paused, smiling at Tom. "Yes, the solution. The master algorithm. You'll need to see this. One of my agents cracked it."

Tom was suddenly tempted to repeat himself—to remind Rodriguez to keep his identity as the code breaker a secret. But Rodriguez was rising to his feet, the phone clamped to his ear, peering at Tom's piece of paper.

"Agent Rodriguez—"

Rodriguez finally looked at him. "Tom, I'm sorry, but I've got to bring this over to cryptography." He had come around the table—now he clapped Tom on the shoulder appreciatively. "A fantastic job, Moore. You've certainly hit the ground running."

"Well—thank you, sir. I'm looking forward to hearing what Oliver's next assignment will be."

"You can see yourself out, can't you, Tom?" Rodriguez said. "I've got to go."

Tom stood there, under the bright fluorescent lights, holding his new CIA badge and feeling rather proud of himself.

He could already picture his brother thanking him—somewhere, someday in the very, very distant future—for freeing him from the shackles of that code. He could picture the day when all their little stresses and misunderstandings had blown over and they could laugh about such trivialities. In fact, he was quite confident that those days were just around the corner.

WHAT COULD HE DO TO FEEL LONELIER?

Bad Idea

That was Oliver's question as he sat stooped over the bar at Chumley's. . . their "place." His and Katia's. Could you even have a "place" with someone who didn't love you? *Probably not,* Oliver thought as he swigged down the remaining scotch in his glass. So what could he do?

He had come here to "their place" so that he could feel her all around him, knowing she was out on her date right this very moment with his brother. All Oliver wanted was to feel lonelier—to drown himself so deep in it that maybe he might finally overload, like an overdriven engine, and then, finally, maybe. . . he'd shut down. That's what he needed right now. To shut down completely. To feel nothing, and think nothing, and most of all, God knew, most of all, to *want* nothing.

Because he wanted her so badly right now. More than he ever had before. More than the first night he'd seen her singing. More than any of those endless nights in the last month when he'd walked her to her

131

door and received his peck on the cheek, starving to know what it was to really kiss her, and to be really kissed by her, and to be on the other side of that door after midnight. Maybe if he had just gotten on the other side of that door once. . .

Oh, please, he scolded himself, actually slapping himself on the back of the head. It was something he and his brother had developed, a quick way to shake off guilt and ill will and demons, just a nice hard smack to your own mismanaged head. But it was no use. The more he thought about himself on the wrong side of that door, the more he thought about his brother on the *right* side of it, touching her the way he never could, the way. . .

"It's the woman, uh?"

The deep voice was just behind Oliver's right ear. He brought his head up from his drink and peered behind him. The man was standing behind his shoulder with an odd, knowing smile.

"Huh?" Oliver grunted. It was the first time he'd actually spoken in the last two hours at the bar. And only now, when he heard himself grunt like a frustrated ape, did he realize how ridiculously drunk he was yet again. Maybe he could make it as a drunk? One could always hope. . . .

"Only a woman can make a man look this way." the man said in a deep Russian accent.

"A woman," Oliver admitted, raising his glass

enthusiastically, trying to slug back the entire glass of scotch. He couldn't quite manage it and was forced to spit a little back in the glass. He placed the glass back down on the bar and wiped a few of the driblets from his chin.

"It is pure injustice," the Russian man said, sitting down on the stool next to Oliver's and ordering himself two shots of vodka. "We both want her," he said, downing the first shot, "and we both can't have her."

"Her?" Oliver asked.

The man turned to him and looked deeper in his eyes. "You don't recognize me?" he asked, each word being swallowed up by his accent.

Oliver tried to bring his vision into better focus. He studied the man's features: his bright red hair, his long, crooked nose, his dark tweed jacket. . . . He'd definitely seen the man before, but apparently tonight he was just a little too drunk. His impeccable instincts as an agent had suffered pretty severely after all that time cooped up in a cramped sublevel office with no windows, staring at miles and miles of numbers every day under horrid fluorescent lighting.

"At the Bitter End," the man said. "I've seen you at almost all the shows, at the front table, uh? Lucky man. Very lucky man. Me, I sit all the way at the back, you know. But still, she is *something*, yes. This Katia. She is something."

Finally a touch of the cloud lifted from Oliver's

head long enough for him to recognize the man. That smiling redhead from the club. The one who gave Katia the creeps. "Indeed she is," Oliver agreed, raising his glass to the man. "She is most definitely *something.*" They clinked glasses and Oliver finished his drink, signaling for his next refill.

"Nikolai," the man said, extending his hand for a shake.

"Oliver," he replied, giving a nice firm handshake.

"A bottle of Stolichnaya," Nicolai said to the bartender. "Two glasses."

The bartender brought the bottle and the glasses, and Nikolai dropped a fifty-dollar bill down on the table. Friendly and quite a tipper.

"We drink, maybe we eat, we talk about Katia."

Oliver couldn't imagine a better offer. He clinked glasses with Nikolai.

"*Nostrovya,*" Nikolai said as they both downed their shots of vodka.

Oliver felt the sting of it going down his throat. And almost immediately he felt a little warmer and a little less depressed.

"You know, Oliver," Nikolai said, pouring them more drinks, "I must admit, I'm a little jealous of you."

"Of *me?*" Oliver scoffed, knowing full well that there was only one Moore brother to be envied right now.

"Yes, you," Nikolai said. "You've gotten to spend so

much time with her. I've watched you two having drinks after her shows, walking through the club arm in arm. I could never get this close to her, you know? I've tried to talk to her, but I could not even get her to say two kind words to me. . . not even two *unkind* words!"

"Yeah, well. . . we're in the same boat now, Nikolai," Oliver said, trying to match him drink for drink.

"How is that?" Nikolai asked.

"I'm out of the picture," Oliver said, feeling a momentary hitch in his throat when he said it. "She's moved on to. . . someone else."

"I don't understand," Nikolai said, giving Oliver a stern glance. "You speak as if this is a permanent state of affairs. As if you will not win her back. Where is your confidence, boy?"

"No," Oliver said. "You don't understand. She never even loved me."

"Well, how do you know this?" Nikolai asked, again with that same stern, almost fatherly expression on his face.

"I know it," Oliver assured him, swerving slightly from side to side now and not minding it so much. "I know it because they never love me, Nikolai. They *never*—"

Nikolai slapped Oliver on the back, stopping him midsentence, and nearly sending his head straight into the table. "Now, you listen to me, Oliver," he said with a new intensity in his voice. "That girl. Our Katia. . . she is a very special girl."

"Oh God, yes," Oliver slurred, nodding emphatically as Nikolai handed him another drink. "She's as special as they come. She's like a moon goddess on a faraway starry—"

"No, no." Nikolai laughed, giving Oliver another hard slap on the back. "I mean, yes, of course, she is *special*, but this is not what I mean. I mean she is a *very special person* to some *very special people*. Katia. She is the *reason* I am in the States right now, you see?"

Oliver tried to understand, but what exactly was there to understand here? "Um. . . no," he uttered slowly.

Nikolai blew out a slight sigh of frustration. "Listen to me," he said. "I think that you and I might be able to *help* each other. We both want her, Oliver. We just want her for very different reasons. But if we *worked together*. . ." Nikolai's grin grew to its largest size yet. "If we worked together, there is no way we wouldn't win her back, do you understand?"

Oliver sat there for a moment, with Nikolai's arm now wrapped around his shoulders and the room spinning in circles. He'd listened very intently to every single word Nikolai had to say, and ultimately, he could come to only one conclusion.

"I have no idea what you're talking about," he said, staring blankly into Nikolai's eyes.

KATIA AND TOM HAD BEEN WALKING

Snow Turtle

and talking for what must have been hours. Since Tom was already somewhat acquainted with Katia's professional pursuits (or in her case, semiprofessional), they spent much of the time discussing Tom's work.

Katia wasn't exactly sure how she felt about the CIA. Since he hadn't actually started yet, his job hadn't been defined. He could end up doing anything, from working at a desk from nine to five, to embarking on dangerous missions. It was too soon to tell. Right now all she knew was how much the job meant to Tom and that she'd secretly cross her fingers and pray for the desk job. And in all honesty, that she was freezing her butt off, which was making it hard for her to think about anything else.

It's your own fault that you're cold, she told herself. *Deal with it, you chicken.*

Yes, it was entirely her fault that she was now shivering rather heavily under her thin coat, fighting to keep her teeth from audibly chattering. Not because she'd never put together the money to buy a decent coat or a pair of gloves. Not because she'd been so damn distracted before the date that she'd neglected to bring her scarf. But for the simple fact that he could have been keeping her warm. He could have been holding her. If she could just bring herself to *touch* him. To let him touch her.

Yes, this "untouchable" problem had most definitely gotten out of hand. And Tom was so inhumanly respectful that he was obviously trying to honor her wishes by keeping his hands in his own pockets as they laughed and stumbled their way down the street, revolving around each other, nearly dancing around each other, aching to get closer, like two armless people in love.

In love. . . Was she definitely in love with—? Oh, shut up. You fell in love with him the second he opened that door. Before he had even opened his gorgeous mouth.

Of course this revelation wasn't without its downside. It meant that Katia had, at least on some level, known about her feelings all along, which meant that for the past month she had been giving Oliver the wrong idea.

Tom had told her that Oliver took the news of their date poorly. And who could blame him? Since the day they met, Katia had spent almost every minute with him and made no effort to be completely honest with him. Because she didn't want to hurt him. Perhaps even because she didn't want to lose him. But also because honesty could be so difficult sometimes.

Take now, for instance. If honesty had factored into Katia's behavior, she would have touched Tom by this point. Or at least allowed him to touch her. Yet every time he so much as brushed against her, she turned to stone, sending him the wrong message again and again, pounding it in with each retracted reach and awkwardly careful passage through a door.

All she knew was that it had something to do with trust. Yes, Katia did not like to admit it to herself, but after everything she had been through back home, trusting men had become a rather complicated issue.

"Do you want to sit?" Tom asked, offering her a spot on a bench that looked out on the dark, moonlit water. Now that they were in Battery Park, they'd pretty much reached the end of the city and could walk no farther.

Katia nodded and sat down, pushing herself up against the steel arm of the wooden bench, keeping her hands in her pockets and trying to duck her head a little farther into her coat.

Tom sat down next to her, looking healthy and red faced from the icy wind as he leaned his elbows on his knees and looked out at the view. The Statue of Liberty was hovering over the water, lit to perfection, the torch shining with a warm amber hue. To the right were the majestic turrets of Ellis Island, wrapped in untended trees, glowing slightly in dark thanks to the rather bright moon.

She could no longer be sure why she was nearly convulsing with shivers. It could have been the freezing cold. It could have been all the gorgeous images of freedom spanning out ahead of her. Or it could have been the mere act of sitting next to him. . . even if she was being absurdly careful not to let her leg even graze against his.

"Oh God, I'm such an idiot," Tom said, suddenly looking back at her. "You're *freezing*. Do you want my coat?" He shot up from the bench and began ripping off his overcoat.

"No," she assured him, speaking through the turned-up collar of her coat. "I'm fine. Keep that on; it's too cold."

Tom held his coat in his hand and looked down at her with a raised eyebrow. "You're telling me you're not freezing right now?"

"I'm *fine*," she insisted, hoping he couldn't hear her teeth chatter when she spoke.

"Fine?" he repeated doubtfully. "You're trying to hibernate inside your coat. You look like a snow turtle."

Katia looked up at him from inside her coat. "Is there such a thing as a snow turtle?"

"I don't *know*." Tom groaned. "Just *take* the coat."

"There's no such thing as a snow turtle," she insisted.

"We can talk about it after you put on the coat. . . up!" he ordered, laughing.

Katia finally rose from the bench, standing too close to him again, with her hands now dug deep under her arms and her eyes locked with his. Tom opened up the coat and draped it behind her shoulders, but as he closed it around her, his hands brushed up under her chin. He snapped them away awkwardly. "Sorry," he uttered quietly, shoving his hands back in his pockets.

"What were you sorry about?" Katia asked.

"Oh—well. . ." he stammered. "Nothing, I just didn't mean to. . . you know. . ."

"To what?"

"To. . ." Tom broke eye contact for a moment, turning out uncomfortably toward the water before turning back to her.

"Okay, this has been one of the greatest nights of my life. . . ." Hearing it made her want to duck farther under the coat and grin like a baby. "I've just," he went on, "I've just gotten this *feeling*. . . even that first day at the bookstore—that. . . you don't want to be touched. Or, you know. . . you don't want to touch me."

And now she felt thoroughly sick. Vomit-level, in-bed-for-days, high-fever-type sick. At least he was as perceptive as she thought he was.

"Which is *fine,*" he added quickly. "I respect that—"

"No," she interrupted him, shaking her head over and over. "No, no, it's not that, Tom. I'm *so* sorry. I should have said something hours ago; I should have said *something.*" She was talking to herself more than him now and absently slapping herself on the head.

"Whoa," he said with a laugh, clamping his strong hand around her wrist before she could get in another shot.

It was the first time he had touched her. The one touch released some nameless chemical through her veins that made the cold simply disappear altogether. And then, just as quickly, he let go.

"*Sorry,*" he said awkwardly. "That was just a reflex."

"No, it's *okay,*" she assured him. "This is my fault, Tom. I can explain it. It's not—"

141

"No," he said quickly, "you don't have to explain it; you don't—"

"No, I *want* to explain it," she insisted. "I. . . are you familiar with the principles of 'untouchability'?"

"What?"

"No, never mind that," she said, looking down at her feet for a moment. Explaining to him that he was too perfect to touch was out of the question. Besides, she'd realized already that it ran a little deeper than that. *All those trust problems. . .*

Maybe you should tell him. Tell him what happened back home. Tell him what you're running from.

"I. . ." she began slowly, avoiding eye contact. "I think maybe. . . I don't trust so easily, Tom."

"Well, sure," he said, "I understand."

"No," she assured him, forcing herself to make eye contact again. "No, you don't understand. Because I haven't explained." The wind flew between their faces, whipping her hair against her cheek and her lips.

"Look," she continued. "There are some things. . . back home in Russia. Some things I had to get away from. . ."

Tom dug his gaze into hers. "Things?" he asked. "Or people?"

"Both," she answered honestly, as she watched the wind snap his short locks of hair back and forth. "And those things. . . and those people," she went on, counting on his steely eyes to carry her through this deeply uncomfortable confession, "they have kind of made me. . . lose faith, you know? So when something is so perfect. . ." *No, that's not what you mean. Say what you mean, Katia.* "When *you* are so perfect," she said, "well, then I don't want to touch you. To touch something is to believe it's real, and then, you know, then one day you find out it isn't."

"I think I understand," he said tentatively.

"And I *do* want to touch you, Tom," she said, feeling her heart leap from her throat and fall to the ground when she said it. She began to feel like either the ground was shaking or her legs might be giving out on her. "And I want *you* to touch *me*." Yes, and now she felt thoroughly sick and light-headed and dizzy. It was all so unexpected. All these crazy fears. God, if only she didn't have all these crazy fears. . .

She dropped back down on the bench and tried to gather herself. But Tom was next to her before she had the chance to harden.

He stared at her profile as she stared out at the water. Now she couldn't even look at him. She was terrified. Terrified that he might try to kiss her. . . but much, much more terrified that he wouldn't.

Thankfully he did.

He cupped her face gently between his two hands, maybe to savor it, maybe to give her a moment's warning. But that was all the warning she would get, and it was all the warning she would need. She craned back her neck and fell into his hands as he pressed his lips to hers, taking in whatever breath she had left—taking every bit of her elation and desire and fear and breathing it in.

And for at least this moment, buried warmly in his arms in the freezing cold, with the wind kicking up off the river and the moon lighting their way, she believed she always could be fearless. As long as they were together. And now she knew that they *would* always be together. They'd be together until the day she died.

"OLIVER. . . MY *FRIEND*," NIKOLAI

Doubtful Whispers

said, with his thickest smile of the night, "I think maybe we are good friends now, uh? Are you my good friend?"

"Well, absolutely!" Oliver agreed, raising his glass high in the air. "You're the best friend I've got, Nikolai!" He downed another vodka shot, barely noticing that the sting of the booze had long since disappeared.

"Shhh." Nikolai laughed, clamping his hand rather forcefully on Oliver's shoulder to quiet him down. "No need to be so *loud*, my good friend."

"Sorry," Oliver slurred. "*Sorry,*" he whispered, proving to his good friend Nikolai that he could in fact whisper if he needed to.

"Good," Nikolai said. "*Much better.*" He slid his chair an inch closer to Oliver's. "So, my friend. . . about working together. . ."

"Yeah, I'm *sorry.*" Oliver laughed, smacking himself on the head. "That just flew right by me. You want to run that whole scenario by me again?"

"Of *course,*" Nikolai offered generously. "I run it by you as many times as you need, my friend. Okay," he began, locking his eyes with Oliver's. "It is like this. I work for some people. Some *very powerful* people. And these people are very interested in Katia, you see? She is extremely important to these extremely important people."

"Uh-huh." Oliver nodded.

"Now, these people," he went on. "They think, and I think, that you could help us. You could help us to win her over, you know? Win over her trust."

"And how would these people know that?" Oliver asked, with a sly drunken smile.

"Well." Nikolai smiled back. "My 'people.' They hang around a lot. They see things. They know things. Maybe I could even say to you, my friend. . . they know *everything.*"

Oliver had suddenly begun to realize what this sounded like. And somewhere way back in the recesses of his head, there was a tiny little sober Oliver that had begun to scream at him, telling him to leave the bar immediately and go find one of his superiors at the Agency and report this. But sober Oliver was miles and miles away. Drunken Oliver could hardly hear his echoing voice so far off in the distance. And right now, in all honesty, the way drunken Oliver was feeling about the Agency, with all their disappointed blank stares and doubtful whispers about his capabilities. . . right now he truthfully didn't care if he was having this conversation or not. Not tonight, he didn't.

He probed Nikolai's eyes dizzily. "I'm too drunk for euphemisms," he admitted. He would just need to ask him point-blank. "Are you KGB?" he asked quietly, trying not to fall off his chair as he leaned forward.

"Good." Nikolai nodded. "The direct approach. I like that. It shows character. Yes, let's be direct, Oliver. This will make things so much clearer. Am I KGB? No. This is what many people believe, and I let them. But I don't work for those bureaucratic dinosaurs. I'd have to be a fool, uh?" Nikolai laughed quietly. "No, my people are far more powerful than KGB. Their intelligence is far superior—in every sense of the word. More powerful than your precious Agency, too, I think."

"Ah, we're not so precious." Oliver laughed. *Stop talking like that!* little sober Oliver was screaming from the bottom of some well in his brain. But he wasn't being serious. He was just playing. He was just blowing off a little resentful steam, that was all.

"You're wiser than I thought." Nikolai grinned.

"You better believe it," Oliver said with not so comic pride. "You want wisdom?" he asked. "Well, how about this. . . I get it. More powerful than the KGB or the CIA? *The Organization*, right? Why don't you just come out with it? You work for the Organization."

No agency knew enough about the Organization to truly understand it. All anyone could really understand was just what Nikolai had said. They seemed to be more powerful than any government agency, maybe for the sole reason that they were *not* a government agency. They seemed to consist entirely of international terrorists and blacklisted agents who'd simply been too smart or too power hungry to stick with the Agency. They were mercenaries, spying for the highest bidder; whether it was the U.S. government or moneyed neo-Nazis, they didn't care. That was what made them so ruthless. They weren't in it for honor or justice or country. They were in it for the money.

"I'm impressed," Nikolai said. "Then you know of us?"

"Know of you?" Oliver huffed. "I've been trying to break one of your damn codes for the last *month*. Who the hell does your encryption? 'Cause he's losing me my goddamn *job*." Oliver drunkenly dropped his head on the table with a self-deprecating laugh. Yes, at this point he'd pretty successfully drowned little sober Oliver in that well deep inside his brain. *Drunkenly joking about national security, Oliver? Jesus, what has happened to you?* But he knew the answer to that. Two things had happened to him. Two things that he could never in a million years have even conceived of happening in his entire young life. (1) He had fallen in love. And (2) he was screwing up his job. He might as well have been another person. On another planet.

He looked back up at Nikolai, who was laughing heartily at his encryption joke. "Yes, well, you see?" Nikolai said. "You'll never solve that code, my friend, because you're on the weaker side. You should come over to our side. Why try to break the codes when you could be *making* them, uh?"

"Yeah." Oliver laughed, too. "Working for a bunch of terrorists and anarchists. Thanks, but no thanks."

"No, but you are missing the point," Nikolai said, finishing his laugh and becoming more serious.

"What's the point?"

Nikolai leaned in much closer, and it was clear that he was done joking. "The point, my friend?" he said. "The point. . . is Katia. We know you want her, and so do we. It is like I said before. We want the *same thing*. And if a man as exceptional as you and an organization as exceptional as ours want the same thing. . . well, if we worked together, how could we possibly not obtain that thing, you see? It's rather foolproof logic, I think."

"What do you mean, *obtain her?*" Oliver asked. "Obtain her *how?* And who are these 'very important people' who are so interested in her?"

"Look. . ." Nikolai began, pouring out what was left of the vodka into Oliver's glass, which Oliver quickly swigged down without thinking. "Have you ever heard of the First Principle?"

Oliver just stared at him blankly. In other words, *no.*

"The First Principle," Nikolai said. "It is the guiding principle of our entire organization. It is how we obtain all of our intelligence and the basis for all of our operations. Let me educate you. The First Principle states that when you have a 'mark,' you must earn that mark's trust *slowly,* you see? You take as much time as necessary to earn their trust fully, and then you have *complete control.* Once you have earned their trust successfully, well, then you can tell *them* what to think, you see? Then you can have whatever it is you want.

"That is why I have been sent here," he went on. "I came to New York to win over Katia's trust. There is only one problem," Nikolai explained, raising his finger in the air like a pompous schoolteacher. "I make her sick." He laughed, drinking down the rest of the vodka in his glass. "You see? I tried to strike up conversations, you know? To get to know her, but *nothing.* It's the same with five or six other of our men, Oliver. Each of them has tried to get a little closer to her. To win her trust, you see? To win her over so that they could deliver her to the interested parties."

Oliver had come to realize that he was never going to hear exactly *who* these interested parties were. What had she gotten herself wrapped up in? It must be something that went back to Russia. All the interested parties were *Russian*. Except, of course, for him. "So we are thinking that is it," he said, raising his arms up in a big shrug. "You, with the perfect American face. You, with the brains and the charm. She *likes* you. I tell this to all my superiors. I tell them I can see it even from the back of the club. *She likes him so much,* I tell them. He could win her trust. He could win her *love,* even."

Oliver would have been lying straight through his very numb teeth if he said he didn't love to hear this. Apparently Nikolai, a complete stranger, could see what Oliver thought he'd been seeing, too. Spy or no spy, he could sense it even from the back of the room. That Katia *was* singing to him when she sang. That she *was* falling for him all those beautiful nights of the last month.

"Now you are beginning to understand, I think." Nikolai smiled, searching deeper in Oliver's eyes. "We need fresh blood, Oliver. A new face with a new perspective. We need an American face. The *perfect American face.* That could be you. A simple deal I'm offering. You help to deliver the girl's trust to my people, and we help to deliver the girl of your dreams to you. Simple."

Oliver's head was swimming. Not just with inhuman levels of alcohol, but also with confusion and resentment and more confusion. He had taken an oath when he joined the Agency. An oath to protect the world against a world of nefarious people just like Nikolai. But goddamn, if the man wasn't offering the one thing Oliver couldn't resist. . . Katia. . . Katia, who should have been with him tonight, at this very moment. . . not out on a *date* with his *brother* after they'd been dating for a *month? Ridiculous! So utterly ridiculous! When did you become such a selfish son of a bitch, Tom?*

But a moment more, and thank God, Oliver's senses snapped back and slapped him in his own face. What the hell was he thinking here? Was alcohol *that* demonic a drug that it could alter one's thinking so completely? Yes, he supposed it was. For a moment there, he had actually felt more connected to a self-proclaimed terrorist than he had to his own twin brother. And that was when Oliver finally remembered exactly where his alliances were. And exactly what insanity looked like. And maybe what it felt like, too.

"God, what the hell am I doing here?" he said finally, staring ashamedly at the empty bottle of vodka and the repulsive little sly smile still pasted on Nikolai's face.

"You are seeing my point." Nikolai laughed, slapping him again on the back. "That's what you are doing. You are recognizing a good thing when you see it."

"Get your hand off me," Oliver slurred, swiping Nikolai's arm off his back. "This conversation is *over*," Oliver stated, standing up out of his chair and using every ounce of his will to maintain his balance. He leaned down and pointed his wobbly finger in Nikolai's face. "I can't believe I was cursing my own brother because of *you*. Of all the pathetic things I've done tonight, that is the worst."

Oliver turned away from Nikolai and started for the door, but Nikolai suddenly grabbed his arm with a surprisingly firm grip and turned Oliver back toward him.

"Your *brother?*" Nikolai scoffed. "Is *that* what's standing in your way of working with us?"

"Let go of me," Oliver insisted, drunkenly debating whether or not to snap his neck with one swift move. It wouldn't be the honorable thing, but what on earth was honorable about Nikolai?

"*Please* tell me you're not that much of a fool." Nikolai snorted. "Believe me, if you want to talk about morality here, then *you* are certainly the one who deserves her. Not him."

"What are you talking about?" Oliver asked in spite of himself. "Let *go* of me." He broke his wrist free of Nikolai's grip, but he didn't walk away. He wasn't sure why. "What do you mean, 'a fool'?" he asked. "Why am I a fool?"

"No," Nikolai said, standing out of his chair. "You are right. Why listen to *me* over *him?* You ask your brother what I mean, Oliver. You don't need to hear about all our surveillance. You ask him. But make sure he tells you the truth this time. Not that nonsense he was giving you in his apartment. '*On my honor as a soldier*' and all that nonsense. Disgusting. Truly disgusting. . ."

Oliver's eyes widened. The Organization had heard

every word in Tom's apartment that morning. Of course, he knew the Agency could bug just about any location they wanted, but this, he just hadn't ever considered this.

"What are you talking about?" Oliver demanded.

"I'm talking about *loyalties*," Nikolai said, staring coldly into Oliver's eyes. "If I told you the truth, you probably wouldn't even believe me. If I told you that your 'noble' brother had been seeing Katia the *entire* time you and she were together, you'd call *me* the liar. If I told you that they never stopped seeing each other since the day they met in that bookstore and that every night when you dropped her at her door nice and early, she would get onto the number one train at Sheridan Square, get off at 110th Street, and spend the night at his house while he *'worked on his thesis'*? Then you would call me a liar, uh? You'd want to punch *me* in the face. But some part of you would *know*, Oliver. You'd hit me, but some part of you would know that every word I just told you was the truth."

"You shut your mouth," Oliver insisted, feeling his entire body simmering with the need for some kind of violence.

"If *this* is why you don't want to make the deal with us, then you truly are a fool, Oliver. Your brother? Loyalty to your brother? Why on earth would you want to be loyal to your brother when he shows absolutely no loyalty to you? When he goes behind your back and sleeps with the woman you love, all the time lying about it to your face?"

"That's enough!" Oliver howled, leaning his face into Nikolai's and clumsily bumping his chest.

"Believe me, Oliver," Nikolai said, "we can show you the infrared videos if you'd like. But I don't think you could stomach them—"

"Shut your mouth, you liar! Stay away from me, do you understand? Stay the hell away from me."

Oliver swiped Nikolai out of his way and ran out of Chumley's and straight toward the river. He had to shake all those lies from his head. Maybe he needed to puke them all out.

Maybe he needed to figure out just how much of it was lies.

It was all he
could do to keep
from fidgeting
in nervous
frustration and
anger. **1983**
He could almost
smell Katia's
perfume all over
his brother.

IT WAS STRANGE, COMING BACK TO
Chumley's the next after-
noon, but Oliver didn't
mind. Right then he
wouldn't have minded
anything because Katia
was meeting him. He
still had a slight head-

Sick Wave of Nothingness

ache from the previous night—his second hangover in a
row. It hurt just badly enough to convince him that he had
been right to swear off drinking, as he had, late last night,
while trying to ward off a bad case of the spins.

He sat by the fireplace with a glass of club soda, feeling
happy—happier than he'd felt, well, in days. Since before
that terrible moment when he turned his head and saw
Tom joining him at the front table at the Bitter End.

The only problem was that he had been told to
report to CIA headquarters for a meeting in the late
afternoon—four hours from now. And he was a bit
nervous about it—he suspected that Rodriguez was
going to press him about his lack of progress with the
Organization's code.

Oliver shrugged that off. After a meeting with Katia,
he would be happy to meet with *five* Rodriguezes.

While waiting, Oliver looked over at the bar and recon-
structed his conversation with Nikolai from the previous
night. He was glad he'd decided to leave before he became
drunk enough to believe Nikolai's stories about Katia.

Each time the door opened, Oliver squinted at the blinding rectangle of daylight, holding his breath, expecting Katia to walk in. But each time it was someone else. He was checking his watch and trying to decide whether to ask for another club soda when he looked up.

And there she was. . .

"Katia!" he called out, waving as he leapt to his feet. She saw him, and her face lit up—she beamed at him as she walked over.

"Hello, Oliver," Katia said warmly. She let her hand rest on his arm as she leaned in to kiss him.

"So, where do you want to go?" Oliver asked excitedly. He had some ideas, actually. Since spending the past month with Katia, he had started noticing restaurants, nightclubs, galleries—all the places that couples went, that he had never paid attention to before.

"Actually, can we just sit here for now? I've been walking all morning."

"Fine, fine," Oliver said, pulling a chair nearer to the fireplace and beckoning the waiter. "I think of this as 'our place,' anyway."

"Really? That's sweet," Katia said. "It's good to see you, Oliver."

"It's great to see you," Oliver said. The waitress had come over—Katia ordered a club soda herself. Which was odd, Oliver thought, since she usually drank white wine—but it was early in the afternoon.

"Listen—I wanted to talk to you," Katia said. She

was leaning forward in the chair, gazing at him from up close. "I want to have a conversation that's a little more serious."

"Okay." Oliver was all ears.

"Oliver, I *really* like you," Katia said. Her eyes told him that she meant it. "The time we've spent together has been so wonderful for me."

"Oh—I feel the same way, Katia."

"I don't even think you fully appreciate what you've done for me," she said. "Before I met you, I was. . . well, I was lonely. I hadn't been in the city very long. . . and I don't even think I realized how closed off I was."

You see, Olly, you had nothing to worry about. You're way too hard on yourself. She does love you. Trust your instincts. Oliver's heart was singing.

"You're a wonderful person, Oliver. A wonderful man. You're generous and warmhearted and smart, and any girl would be—well, she'd be lucky to get you, that's all."

"Thanks," Oliver said, feeling his cheeks heat up. "I mean, you're too kind. I'm not all those things."

"You *are,*" Katia said urgently. She had reached to touch his hands as she looked at him. "You are. And you need to *believe* that you are—to have confidence that a woman can see your goodness in your eyes."

"Can you see it?" Oliver asked.

But Katia had cast her eyes down—she was staring at the bubbles rising through her club soda.

"Oliver," she said, more slowly, "that's why this is

so difficult for me. I have to say something that I don't want to—and I need to know you're really listening."

"W—what? I mean, yes. I'm listening."

A knot of wood exploded in the fireplace suddenly—the popping noise made them both jump. Katia pulled her hands away from his, laughing nervously.

"Oliver," Katia said, "I'm in love with Tom. Tom and I—Tom and I are involved now."

It actually took a full five seconds for Oliver to absorb what she'd said. He was staring at her dully, feeling a knot forming in his stomach.

He could barely move.

"Wait," he finally said. "In *love*—so *soon?* I mean, it's been—you've only had one date!"

"Oliver," Katia said. "That's something else you need to understand. I mean, I barely understand it myself—"

"What? What are you trying to tell me?" Oliver said harshly. Someone at the bar glanced over—he was speaking more loudly than he'd intended.

"Tom and I—our love really began the day we met," Katia said quietly. "In the bookstore. We've been 'involved,' if you want to put it like that, since that day."

And now she finally looked at him, and tears ran down her face. "I'm sorry I wasn't honest about that, Oliver. I never talked about him. But I've loved him since the moment we met."

Oliver stared back at her the way one would stare

at an oncoming train before it hit you—when it was too late, when you were powerless to get out of the way. That was the only thing he could compare it to in his mind. It was that bad.

"So you've lied to me," he managed to say.

"Oh, Oliver, *no*," Katia said, wiping her eyes. "No. I guess I've—I'm just so sorry."

"Uh-huh," Oliver said. He was staring at the bar, where he and Nikolai had drunk all that vodka just a day before. "You're sorry."

"Oliver—"

"A *month* of lying! Both of you!" He couldn't believe it. Nikolai had been right. *On my honor as a soldier,* he thought bitterly. *Tom, you bastard.*

Maybe *everything* Nikolai had said was correct.

"Where are you going?" Katia asked. Her untouched drink stood on the table, reflecting the bright firelight. Oliver realized he had risen to his feet.

"I've got to go," he said, stumbling forward.

Oliver made it past her, without knocking the chairs over, without touching her, and stumbled toward the door of Chumley's for the second time in as many days. As he yanked on the wooden door and came out into the sun, he realized he was crying, but he wasn't feeling the release of his tears—he felt a terrible, empty pain in his stomach, and at the same time he felt nothing, a sick wave of nothingness that was somehow worse than the pain.

"THANKS FOR COMING IN," RODRIGUEZ

Dangerously Close

said, leaning on the conference room table. "I wanted you both here so I could go over some organizational changes."

Organizational changes? Oliver thought.

He was sitting next to Tom, and it was all he could do to keep from fidgeting in nervous frustration and anger. He could almost smell Katia's perfume all over his brother. And with Rodriguez there, Oliver was trapped—there was nothing he could do or say right now that wouldn't jeopardize his career.

And that was what he focused on. Oliver stared straight ahead at Rodriguez, concentrating on the room, which he'd been in countless times, and on Rodriguez, his superior, whom he'd spoken to time and time again. Oliver felt at home here—in a way Tom clearly did not. He hadn't missed the way that Tom looked around like a tourist as they came down the corridor together.

Did I really want us both to work here? Oliver thought wonderingly. *Was that really my game plan? To have Tom right next to me in the same job?*

Sliding his eyes sideways to look at Tom, Oliver decided that it was a bad idea—that it had always been a bad idea. Why couldn't Tom have stayed at the university, where he belonged? Why didn't he get out of here—and go do something useful, like actually *write* his thesis, rather than use it as a cover while secretly seducing Oliver's girl?

"The agency places a tremendous value on each of you," Rodriguez was saying, looking back and forth between them. "These new changes reflect that. Oliver, you've been heading up our code division for the past few years—and you've done some extraordinary work there."

Until now, Oliver thought. He had a sudden fear that he was about to be reprimanded. *That's what this is about*, he thought nervously. He could feel a thin film of cold sweat breaking out on his forehead—he wanted to wipe it away, but he thought that would be too obvious. *Rod's going to dress me down but good for failing to crack that damn code.*

"Recently you've run into some trouble," Rodriguez went on. Oliver felt a sinking feeling. *Here it comes*, he thought. "The intercepted Organization message. You haven't been able to crack it."

The Organization. Right then Oliver's fear began to combine with a different feeling entirely. He began to feel a crazy sort of guilt, as if he was getting away with something. Because he hadn't said anything about Nikolai.

He *knew* he should be reporting his encounters with Nikolai. He should be telling Tom and Rodriguez all about their meetings, recalling every detail so that it could go into a case file. Nikolai's card, which Nikolai had given him at the bar and which Oliver still had in his pocket, should have already been handed over to Rodriguez and placed in an evidence bag to be analyzed by the CIA lab technicians. Nikolai's clothing, his habits, his promises, all of his talk about the Organization and Katia—he should already be reporting all of it.

But he couldn't do it. There was no way to sit there and tell Rodriguez about Katia. Not with Tom sitting right there. It would have to wait. So he said nothing and kept listening, waiting for the reprimand he knew was coming.

I'll just have to suck it up this time, he told himself. *Once I break the code, I'm sure all will be forgiven. From now on I'll just drown myself in work rather than booze. To hell with Nikolai and everyone else.*

"Well, I've got some good news, Oliver." Rodriguez was smiling at him. "Going forward, you won't have to worry about cracking that code."

"What?" It wasn't at all what Oliver was expecting to hear. "Why not?"

"Because it's been solved," Rodriguez said, grinning. He had produced a file folder and was handing it over. *Encryption Project,* Oliver read on the spine, followed by the previous day's date.

"But—I don't understand," Oliver said finally. He was staring at the file folder, thinking about Nikolai, thinking about Katia, thinking about his throbbing head. Tom was sitting next to him, staring straight ahead—no doubt thinking about his sexy new girlfriend. But Rodriguez had Oliver's full attention. This was completely confusing. The code was *solved?* Since *when?* Who had solved it?

"The changes are as follows," Rodriguez was saying. "Oliver, since your main project is now complete, we're going to move you over to the robotics division. It'll be a fresh start for you since the agency feels you've, uh, outlived your usefulness in code breaking."

"What?" Tom sat forward suddenly. "Wait, that's not what we agreed. You can't just take him off the—"

"Robotics?" Oliver repeated. "I'm sorry, I don't understand, Agent Rodriguez. Who cracked the code?"

"Your father was a programmer in the seventies, wasn't he?" Rodriguez said. Oliver was struggling to follow the logic of what he was saying. *My father?* "I'm not surprised, given the genes he's passed on. Since your brother, Tom, managed to crack the code, we're going to put him in charge of the code-breaking team."

"Put him in *charge?*" Oliver repeated weakly. "What?"

"That's not what we agreed!" Tom yelled, leaning forward on the conference table. "Damn it, Rodriguez, you weren't even supposed to—"

"You stole my job, you—" Oliver was staring at Tom incredulously. He still couldn't believe it. He had expected something bad, but *this*—he wouldn't have believed it in a million years, even as a hypothetical. Tom was actually being given *his* job.

"Oliver," Tom said urgently, grabbing Oliver's arm.

"You've got to believe me. This is a complete misunderstanding. I'm not trying to. . . He wasn't supposed to—"

"*Don't touch me,*" Oliver said quietly. He was planning on keeping this quiet. Agent Rodriguez was across the table, and that meant this would stay quiet. Rodriguez had been duped somehow—he had fallen into Tom's trap, with this nonsense about the code being solved. Rodriguez, Katia—they were all the same in the end. All victims of Tom's charms.

"Oliver—"

"I said *keep your hands off me,*" Oliver said even more quietly. The perspiration was now pouring off his face. His hands, under the table, were clenched into fists, with the thumbs pulled taut, for maximum damage when they hit flesh. *I can take them both,* he thought. *Easily.*

"Oliver, look," Rodriguez said. "This may not be exactly what you wanted, but I assure you that robotics is a perfectly—"

"*Go to hell,*" Oliver said venomously. He rose to his feet so quickly that the metal chair flew backward, colliding with the wall. The clatter of the chair was shockingly loud in the small room. "Both of you!"

Oliver was dangerously close to dropping into a fighting stance— which would have been a big mistake since he'd still have to make his way out of a building full of CIA agents. Thankfully he realized this in time—just before he yanked open the door and, eyes blinded by tears, ran from the room.

You can all go to hell.

You, Tom, with your reassuring smiles, and your "soldier's honor," and the rabbits you keep pulling out of hats—the broken codes, all the girls.

And *you*, Agent Rodriguez—you can go to hell, too. Sending me to the robotics division, of all places.

And Katia—dear, sweet, deluded Katia. What did he do to you to make you believe his lies? There have been so many girls, Katia. Just wait—you'll find out what he's really like.

But you nailed it, Katia, darling, didn't you? This afternoon. I need to *believe* that I'm wonderful, you told me. *To have confidence that a woman can see your goodness in your eyes.* Well, get ready to look into my eyes, Katia, and see just that. I'm finished with being weak.

You want to see what I'm *really* capable of? I'll show you what I'm really capable of.

OLIVER COULDN'T BELIEVE WHAT

His Own Man

he was doing—but at the same time there was a peculiar rightness to it. He was finally doing something for himself. He wasn't a pawn in someone else's game—in Rodriguez's game, or Tom's, or Katia's—anymore.

He pulled the card out of his pocket. *This is it*, he thought, looking up at the industrial building in front of him. *The Organization*.

This was espionage gold—the location of the Organization's Manhattan headquarters. All he had to do was get back on the subway, head uptown, and report.

And then what? he thought, standing there at the doorway. *The robotics division?* Hardly an appetizing thought.

And don't forget Tom. That was the other part—he would spend days, months—years—watching his upstart twin brother run the code division. And every time Tom came in late to work, Oliver would have to imagine him lingering at home with Katia, making puppy-dog eyes at her across the breakfast table in that awful messy apartment of his.

No, he thought. He had made up his mind. There was no going back now.

Standing up straight, he knocked on the door.

With an electronic buzzing noise, the door opened. Nikolai was standing there.

"Welcome, my friend," Nikolai said warmly. "Won't you come in?"

The brothers
were closer
now than
they had
been since
long before 1983
this whole
conflict
over girls
and codes
had begun.

IT WAS THE END OF MARCH AND

Gloved Hands

the beginning of spring. All over New York, the ice had melted. The air was getting warmer, and buds were appearing on the trees. Tom had his window open, and the warm air was blowing into his apartment, rustling the covers of magazines and newspapers that were piled around the room. Outside the window, the sky was fading from bright blue to a deeper gold.

He tried to remember the story of how his father proposed to his mother. The story wasn't complicated. Tom and Oliver's father had always told it in a quiet, shambling voice. They had gone to the nicest restaurant he could afford. He had the ring in his pocket the whole time, but he kept checking for it with his fingers every five minutes. He was convinced their mother had seen him doing it and was on to him the entire night. But she always insisted that she had no idea. She was shocked, she said later, but at the same time it was like she had known all along, that day, from the first time their eyes had met.

Now Tom was doing the same thing. The ring was in his pocket. He checked it again. He was tying his tie over and over—it always came out slightly crooked—and wondering whether or not to shave. Not that he *hadn't* shaved, exactly, but it hadn't turned out to be a terribly *close* shave. He looked a little stubbly. On the other hand, he didn't really have time to undo his tie and shave again. Checking his watch, he took a deep breath, held it, and blew it out, nodding at his reflection in the bathroom mirror. It was time to stop playing games and just go propose.

Walking out onto Morningside Drive, Tom checked his pocket for the ring again. He had it—the small velvet case brushed against his fingers. If everything went right, he thought, Katia would be pulling open that box at eight-thirty, just as Tom signaled the waiters to bring the champagne. And then, at a quarter to nine, Oliver would arrive. That was the other surprise he had planned.

If he was going to be married, then he would be needing a best man, and after everything he and Oliver had been through in the past weeks, it meant the world to Tom to have his brother back by his side, celebrating his love for Katia instead of resenting it. Tom had honestly begun to doubt whether that kind of family bond could ever exist again.

The truth was, Oliver's suffering had hurt Tom terribly. He didn't fully understand what had upset his brother so much. He knew that Oliver had spent an important, meaningful time with Katia—but it had torn into him somehow and caused the rage and fear that had blazed from Oliver's eyes that terrible day he ran out of the Agency. That night Tom lay awake, confused and troubled by his brother's strong emotions. He had tried to call him, leaving message after message and getting no reply. Tom had finally decided that Oliver would have to come around on his own—but Oliver had surprised him. The change had come much more quickly than Tom had expected. It had only been a couple of days before Oliver was apologizing for his "immature behavior" and promising to heal the rift he'd created between them.

The brothers were closer now than they had been since long before this whole conflict over girls and codes had begun. The rift was healed.

That was why Tom had invited Oliver to join them tonight—to celebrate that healing, to mark the beginning of a new and peaceful life between the three of them.

And Katia didn't know about any of it—he had managed to keep everything secret. She had agreed to meet him at the Four Seasons, and that was all she knew.

Tom kept picturing the wedding, though he was trying not to let himself do it too often. After all, Katia hadn't even said yes yet. So he thought about little pieces of it at a time. Right now he was imagining Katia walking down the aisle, her glowing face shrouded in white netting, holding her breath and leaning in toward Tom as she approached him at the altar. He then extended his arm toward her. . .

"*Ugh*—"

A brutally powerful blow crashed against the side of Tom's head.

What was that?

Tom's vision blacked out for a second and he saw stars. But it took less than a second for him to react.

Attack, he barely registered. *I'm being mugged. Jesus, not tonight, New York. Please, not tonight. . .*

At least two people had attacked—he could tell from the angles of the blows. Blood was pouring from a gash near his ear, running into his eyes. He could see someone's feet, and he kicked out without thinking, feeling the blow connect. The shock traveled up his leg.

He had to get out of this. He had to get out of it *now.*

They didn't understand who they were dealing with here. His Green Beret training was kicking in—telling him to stand. It was very important, being upright. There was no way to fight properly from the ground. But a series of hammerlike blows were landing on him.

How many of them are there?

A sharp blow cracked against his shoulder, sending agony down his arm. His hand wouldn't move. He was being hit with wooden clubs. This wasn't a mugging; it was just a full-force beating. Pumped full of adrenaline, Tom got up on his knees, trying desperately to see his attackers. There were definitely three men—now that he was standing, he could see that they wore gray suits, black gloves, and black stockings pulled over their faces. He couldn't tell if they were trying to kill him or not. Assassins wouldn't do this—they used bullets. Were they taking him prisoner? What did they want? He couldn't tell, and already he was feeling faint. The suit he wore was coming apart, the wedding ring in its box toppling to the dirty ground and rolling out of reach. *No. . . !*

He stretched his fingers out desperately for the ring, but dark spots were blooming before his eyes. The blows had stopped. The world was graying out.

Katia, Tom thought weakly.

Gloved hands grabbed Tom's wrists and ankles. They picked him up. He was being carried somewhere by men barking orders at each other, but Tom couldn't hear them through the ringing in his ears.

Where are they taking me?

They swung him back and forth. Then he went flying through the air. *This is going to hurt,* he thought dazedly. There was a muffled thud as he landed in a soft, wet pile of—what? He couldn't tell.

Dumpster, Tom registered barely. *I'm in a Dumpster.*

He tried to move, but it was impossible. He was in way too much pain to think straight. To his relief, all sound began to fade as darkness rolled over him like black fog.

The Big Mistake

"WOULD THE LADY CARE FOR ANOTHER glass of wine?" the waiter asked.

"No—I'm fine, thank you," Katia said.

She had never been to the Four Seasons before—

I don't fit in here, she had

thought, walking in. *They can tell I don't belong.*

And it *had* felt like that at first. When the waiter pulled out her chair, it scraped the floor and made a loud noise, and Katia was convinced that the entire restaurant was staring at her.

But then after a few minutes—after the waiter brought a glass of the best Chablis she'd ever tasted—Katia felt a little less conspicuous.

So where is he? Katia thought after waiting ten minutes. Tom almost never made her wait. But then, Tom always told her what his plans were—or asked what *she* wanted to do. Tonight was different. Tonight he had created a bona fide mysterious evening. He had told her where to meet him and then smiled that maddening, beautiful smile and kissed her on the mouth.

She kept sipping her wine. She tried not to look at her watch too often. When she finally looked a second time, an hour and a half had passed.

At first she had just figured that Tom had been held up. *It's the job,* she had told herself. *It's the subway. It's a cab. It's an accident ahead of him—the traffic is stalled.*

It's an accident and he's in it.

Katia tried to pretend she hadn't thought that. She stared straight ahead. Other couples were looking at her. They were pretending not to, but they were all glancing over. And who could blame them? It was obvious what was going on. A lady didn't get all dressed up for dinner at one of New York's most expensive, most elegant restaurants to dine alone. And even if she did, Katia thought, her annoyance growing, she would *eat* something, wouldn't she? Rather than just sit by herself for more than an hour and a half, nursing a single glass of wine. No, it was painfully clear what was going on.

At a quarter to nine she'd had enough. He wasn't coming. It was as simple as that. And it hurt. It hurt so much more than she would have expected it to. Because it reminded her of the first night at the Bitter End—the first time he'd stood her up. Of course that all had been explained to her, but the feeling, the emotion of being stood up, never went away.

She located the waiter—he was off to one side, pouring champagne for another table, some happy couple fawning over each other, which only made her more angry—and when she got his eye, she signaled for the check.

This wasn't the way the evening was supposed to go, Katia thought as she pulled the balled-up dollar bills out of her purse. She checked to make sure she had enough, and the crumpling of the money seemed to attract everyone's attention again. All she had was eighteen dollars, which she handed over, in full, to the waiter on his silver tray. Ten dollars for the drink, eight dollars' tip to make up for monopolizing the table for so long.

Except for the two quarters in her purse, Katia was broke. She'd have to persuade her cab driver to wait for her while she went into the flower shop on the corner to persuade the proprietor or his daughter to lend her fifteen dollars for the fare.

The coat check lady handed Katia her coat, smiling sympathetically, and Katia had to force herself not to slap the woman in the face with her purse. Everyone was now staring. *Yes, people. I'm the girl who was stood up. Get a good look. Be sure to catch the second show at midnight!*

She stepped through the restaurant's glass doors out into the cool night air and surveyed the crawling traffic on Fifth Avenue, trying to find an empty taxicab.

"Well, hello again, my lovely young friend," an all-too-familiar, accented voice rasped behind her. Katia felt every muscle in her body recoil in revulsion. No, not just revulsion. . . fear.

"Don't you look nice tonight," the creepy voice said.

It was *him*. The troll-like, redheaded weasel. God, he really *was* following her.

This she hadn't expected. She knew he was slimy. She knew he'd come to a few of her shows at The Bitter End, but she hadn't known he was a full-fledged stalker.

And she hadn't thought she'd ever find herself alone with him. . . on a virtually deserted street. . . at night.

"Get. . . get away from me," Katia muttered, walking as quickly as possible.

"So rude," he said, catching up with her as she walked.

"Please," she uttered. "Please just—"

"'Please'?" he interrupted. Katia could see how

yellow and dirty his teeth were—he was close enough for her to notice his dry, pale skin and watery eyes.

Oh God, she prayed to herself silently. *Please don't let this be how I go. I left Russia to escape the men like this in my life. You can't be that cruel, God.*

She checked around her; there was nowhere to go. She wasn't in a bookstore or a crowded bar. She was on a wide limestone plaza, in Midtown Manhattan, on a chilly spring night, with absolutely no one around. And she was wearing high heels—not exactly the best footwear for running away.

"Okay. . . look," she said finally, with a crack in her voice that she quickly tried to cover. "Look, I'm. . . sure you're. . . very nice. But I'm really not—I'm not interested. Please don't bother me anymore."

"Bother you?" The man smiled at her—and there was something very odd about the smile. "I have not *bothered* you. Not at all."

Suddenly Katia noticed something. In the shadows, in the courtyard of the adjacent building, something was moving. It was a man—a man in a gray suit.

"If I wanted to *bother* you," he told her, "I would need some help, I think."

The gray-suited man was getting closer. For the first time since leaving the Four Seasons, Katia was afraid.

"Oh, you needn't mind Boris," he said, referring to the gray-suited man. His yellow teeth caught the light as he smiled. He was close enough that she could smell his sour breath. "Boris is not going to hurt you—unless, of course, you make me angry."

Katia's heart raced.

"W—what do you want?" Katia was trying to keep her balance as she backed away from the man, but she was beginning to stumble. The other man was circling toward her, his arm slightly raised. The closer he got, the easier it was for Katia to see how *big* the man was, like the soldiers she'd seen in Leningrad as a girl.

"What do you *think* I want?" the man said, grinning. Right then Katia lost her balance on the smooth stones.

"Whoops! Watch your step," said a familiar voice behind her.

Katia almost cried out in relief as strong hands caught her shoulders, helping her back on her feet. She'd never thought she could *ever* be so grateful to hear that wonderful, brave American voice.

"Are you all right?" Oliver asked, looking down at her. His face was full of genuine concern.

"*Oliver*—thank God," Katia said. "Yes, I'm fine," she told him gratefully.

Oliver nodded quickly and turned his eyes toward the redheaded weasel.

"Listen, why don't you clear out of here?" Oliver told the man. "I don't think the lady's interested."

Oliver had a strong, protective arm around Katia's shoulders. She was leaning gratefully against him. "I'm sorry," Oliver murmured to Katia, pressing gently on her shoulders. "I have to let go of you for a second, okay?"

Katia stood up straight. As Oliver stepped away from her, she happened to glance over at the man in the gray suit—and she caught a glimpse of something flashing. It was a bright glitter of steel. *"He's got a knife!"* Katia screamed to Oliver. *"Look out!"*

Katia saw Oliver glance at her with a flick of his eyes to check if she had regained her balance. And then he stepped casually forward. His hands were at his sides. And she saw something in his eyes—something she never forgot.

In Oliver's eyes, she saw no fear at all.

The man in the gray suit suddenly lunged at Oliver, leading with the oversized steel bowie knife. Katia heard the leather of his shoes sliding on the granite. And then something amazing happened.

Never in her entire life had Katia ever seen anyone move so fast. She watched incredulously as Oliver darted forward, reaching past the knife to grab the gray-suited man's wrist. Somehow he pulled the knife hand downward while he elbowed the man's gut and arched backward to kick him in the head. It barely registered that Oliver was even moving before it was over and the man was on the ground, unconscious. The knife clattered onto the granite at Oliver's feet.

The weasel swung his arms around, his eyes widening, and then he lost his balance and fell on the plaza's paving stones.

Katia hadn't seen Oliver touch him—but he *must* have, she thought, because he was bleeding, and he'd fallen very heavily on the stones.

How could she have ever thought of Oliver as weak? Had she ever misperceived someone so completely? He had done something that would have been difficult or impossible for most Olympic athletes, and he had done it faster than her eyes could see.

"Are you all right?" Oliver asked, smiling shyly over at Katia.

He isn't even winded, Katia noted. The weasel and his gray-suited accomplice were still lying on the pavement, practically in a heap.

"I'm fine," Katia told him. "*Thank you,* Oliver. I just. . . I can't believe your perfect timing. I really thought I was going to. . . well, thank God you were here."

"What do you mean, 'timing'?" He looked at her in genuine surprise. "Weren't you expecting me?"

"What?"

"Tom invited me." He was guiding her toward the wide, shallow steps on the side of the plaza, away from the two men lying on the pavement. "Show up for dessert at the Four Seasons. Didn't he tell you?" Oliver looked around. "Where *is* he, anyway?"

"I don't *know,*" Katia yelled out, all her frustration and fear finally released. "I don't know. I've been waiting for *hours,* and he didn't even *call.* And if you hadn't been here now, I probably would have been. . ."

And the tears finally came. She reached out for Oliver, pulling him against her. She couldn't stop herself from shaking, as hard as she tried.

"Shhh," Oliver said. "It's okay."

He pulled away from her and smiled—that humble, gentle smile that was so different from Tom's brazen grin. "Are you sure you're all right? You want me to take you home?"

"Well—" Katia was wiping her eyes, trying to put this whole miserable night behind her. "If it's not too much trouble."

"No trouble at all," Oliver said. He was smiling again.

How many
times had he
done this?
How many
evenings had
ended right   **1983**
here, with
the kiss on
the cheek and
the closing
door?

"JUST PULL UP RIGHT HERE, DRIVER,"

Like Clockwork

Oliver said.

He and Katia were in the backseat of a yellow taxicab, slowly driving down Jane Street. So far, everything had gone perfectly, Oliver thought. The First Principle was a *very* effective weapon. It had taken only a few weeks to get here—to be sitting next to her again.

He was being careful not to look at her. If he looked at her, he might lose his composure—and say the wrong thing. He couldn't let that happen. He had worked too hard, and suffered too much, to get to where he was tonight.

First he had worked on winning Rodriguez back.

"Trust is easy to win—if you are willing to make sacrifices," Nikolai had lectured him. "Begin with this Rodriguez. You will learn how easy it can be. You need only throw everything else away—your pride, your devotion to telling the truth, your faith in the goodness of other people. And once you are free of those weaknesses, you can win *anyone's* trust."

Oliver had carefully planned his approach—and then had gone into the CIA and spent forty minutes lying to Agent Rodriguez. He looked directly into the agent's eyes, trying not to think about how much he detested him, and apologized for his outburst that horrible day, explaining how tense he had been and

183

how sorry he was for losing his composure. Then he affirmed his deep, newfound commitment to robotics.

And it worked. Rodriguez had signed the transfer papers, smiling at Oliver in genuine relief. There was a small potential for setback when Oliver happened to glance down at Rodriguez's desk, where he saw another transfer form. With a sudden stab of anger, reading upside down, Oliver saw that it read, *Tom Moore, Senior Director, Coding and Encryption Division.* It had taken a moment of furious effort to keep Rodriguez from seeing the rage on his face.

And he was getting better at that with each passing moment. Before he knew it, Rodriguez was welcoming him back to the CIA active duty roster.

"You see?" Nikolai had beamed at him in delight, cracking the seal on a fresh bottle of Stolichnaya vodka. "You *can* do it. You have won Rodriguez back—and your feet are firmly planted on the road to winning *Katia* back. The feeling of seeing the results with your own eyes, it's exhilarating, no?"

It was.

Next he turned his attentions from Rodriguez to Tom—and the more he apologized, the more Tom responded with relief and sympathy, his concern and mistrust fading away. It was harder to play this role—Oliver had to make Tom forget the raging hatred spewing out of him the day of the meeting with Rodriguez. It was almost physically painful to endure Tom's condescension as he shamelessly exploited their "brotherly" rapport to keep Oliver from noticing all the ways he was taking advantage of him. Oliver listened, almost trembling with frustration—and thought furiously about the "First Principle." But each step closer to Tom was a step closer to Katia. Thinking that way, he could make himself do it. Imagining Katia's soulful brown eyes and her long, soft hair, he could stare right back at Tom and not even blink.

And today it had all paid off. Tom called and invited Oliver to the Four Seasons for dessert with the happy couple.

The evening's tricks had succeeded. Nikolai's henchmen had quickly neutralized Tom, according to their report on the transceiver. Later, Oliver's fight with Boris and the move that had taken Nikolai down (which they had choreographed carefully to make sure Oliver didn't hurt him too badly) went like clockwork.

There was just one unforeseen complication.

It was Katia. Oliver hadn't been prepared for the effect of being near her again. She was just so beautiful. His first glimpse of her had taken his breath away. When he reached out and took her firm, bare shoulders in his hands, he wondered how he had possibly made it so long without being near her. And with each passing minute, as he summoned a cab to take her downtown, his desire for her grew.

And grew. When he opened the door to help Katia out of the taxicab, the slit in her skirt revealed her long, slim thighs for a moment. Then, as she took his hand, smiling at him, he nearly lost it.

"Thanks," Katia said.

"What? Oh, don't mention it," Oliver said carelessly.

And now they were at the doorway. Katia's doorway—the brown-painted wooden doorway with the brick steps leading up to it and the old fashioned brass lamps on either side. He remembered it well.

"Are you all right?" Oliver asked, his voice full of concern. "Are you feeling better?"

"Much better," Katia said, still smiling at him. "Thanks, Oliver." And she reached to squeeze his arm.

As Katia climbed the steps, Oliver followed. How many times had he done this? How many evenings had ended right here, with the kiss on the cheek and the closing door? And the long walk home, alone. . .

This would be the last time.

Katia opened her handbag and pulled out her key. She brushed her hair away from her face as she did it, and Oliver yearned to touch it himself. He imagined brushing it back and leaning to kiss her, really kiss her, for the first time. Her back was to him, and she couldn't see him clench his eyes shut just for a second.

"Listen," Katia said, turning to face him. "Do you want to come inside?"

"What?"

"Do you want to come in and have some tea? I don't think I can go to sleep just yet."

And staring into Katia's eyes, Oliver almost faltered. He almost lost sight of the master plan, the First Principle that Nikolai had explained to him time and time again. He could get lost in her eyes all over again every time he saw her. It was inevitable.

He put on his "honest smile" again.

"No," Oliver said awkwardly. "No, I don't think so. It's late. Thanks anyway, though."

"Are you sure?" Katia said, stepping closer to him. "You saved my life, Oliver. And I've *missed* you. The least I can do is give you a cup of tea."

"Well—" Oliver shrugged, his hands in his pockets, gazing away down the street. "I'm not sure it's, um, appropriate, you know? I mean, you're Tom's girlfriend."

"Is that what I am?" Katia asked, putting her hand on Oliver's arm. "Come on Oliver. Come inside."

"No," Oliver said. "No—thanks, Katia. I've got to get home. I've got—I've got to get to work early tomorrow. Some other time."

"All right," Katia said, frowning. She looked perplexed. "All right. Good night, Oliver."

And then Katia leaned forward to kiss Oliver's cheek—but he wasn't there. He had stepped away, down the brick steps and onto the sidewalk. He kept walking, not looking back.

She's still there, Oliver thought, walking down

Jane Street. *All I have to do is turn around and go back.*

The First Principle was *working.*

He was winning her back.

TOM'S SUIT WAS TORN AND STAINED.

His face was bruised and smeared with blood, and his head and neck were battered and dirty. Passengers on the express train had backed away from him, their noses wrinkled in disgust. He looked awful, and he smelled like rancid Chinese restaurant garbage—

Safe Harbor

but there had been no time to do anything about it. He needed to get to Katia as fast as he could.

He was almost certain that the attack had been orchestrated to get him out of the way—it was the only explanation that made any sense—and it terrified him to think about what that could mean in terms of Katia's safety. He had been unconscious for nearly two hours—until the memory of the ring falling out of his pocket roused him out of his stupor. Enough time for anything to have happened to her, anything he could think of.

In a panic-induced adrenaline rush, Tom found the ring. It had rolled under a parked car. Now, arriving on Jane Street, he could finally see it to safe harbor.

Tom raced up Katia's brick steps. The street door usually was latched, but now it was propped open, which made Tom apprehensive. Had someone from the Organization been here earlier? Was he too late?

"Katia?" he called out. His injured hand stung with every loud knock on the door. "Katia!" he called out again. "Katia? Are you there?"

"Tom?" Her troubled voice came from behind the door. "Tom, is that you?"

Tom sank against the smooth surface of the door, his eyes closed, sighing in overwhelming relief. He hadn't realized just how frightened he had been until that moment.

"Katia, are you all right—?"

She'd swung open the door before he could even finish his sentence. Her brow seemed furrowed with anger, but there was a desperate brand of concern in her eyes. And then she took him in—all the bruises on his face, his dirt-clotted, messy hair, his torn and stained suit— and her expression melted into a stricken look.

"Oh my God, Tom—what *happened* to you?" She dragged him in through the doorway and sat him down on the couch.

"It's, um—it's a long story," he told her. He was staring into her eyes as if he couldn't believe it was actually her.

"Do those—do those hurt?" She was reaching up gently to touch his face.

"What? A little bit," Tom said. "It's nothing, really. I *tried* to get down here as fast as I could, Katia; I'm sorry I got delayed—"

"No, no—" She was shaking her head. "Tom, what happened to your face? Who did this?"

"I can't. . . I really don't know. . . ."

"Tom." She groaned anxiously. "This isn't *fair*. You can't just. . . I was worried sick about you tonight, do you know that? Worried sick about both of us."

"What does that mean—?"

"And now look at you," she interrupted, beginning to talk a mile a minute. "This job, Tom, what you do, I can't live like this. Not knowing if you're going to come home some night looking like *this*. Not even knowing if you're going to come home at all. Soon I won't be breathing at all—I'll be holding my breath, wondering why you didn't show for dinner, holding my breath, wondering where you are at every moment, whether or not you're safe. I need to know where you are, Tom. I need to know you're coming home—"

"Shhh." Tom placed his aching hands on her face, now wet with sudden tears, and tried to quiet her. "It's okay. I *know*." He reached down and began fumbling in his pocket. "That's why I'm here. I want to—"

"I can't live in constant doubt."

"That's my point, Katia." He touched her arm; she flinched. "Look at me."

She finally moved her eyes, looking into his. They

were very close now, and he brought the velvet box out of his pocket.

"That's my point," he repeated, eye to eye with her. "That's what I came down here to say. I want to be there for you from now on, Katia."

Was this how you did it, Dad? he thought, remembering the story as he raised the box and opened it. *Did it feel like this?*

Katia looked at Tom's hands and saw the box. It took her a second.

"Oh, Tom—" Katia uttered. She had reached up to touch his hand gently.

"Katia," Tom said, opening the box so she could see the ring, "will you marry me?"

The ring was important. They always told you that, the people who gave advice. Even Tom's father talked about the ring. The diamond was supposed to be the keystone of the moment, the rock-hard proof of love and commitment.

But this wasn't like that. Neither of them was looking at the ring. It could have easily dropped to the floor, and no one would have noticed.

Tom and Katia were staring at each other, and it was like they were back in the bookstore, that cold day long ago, when all she had wanted was a quiet place to write in her journal and all he'd wanted was to be done with his thesis.

"Yes," she said. That was all. Just "yes." But that was all he needed.

He blew out the breath he had been holding,

slumping his shoulders; he leaned forward, and his dirty forehead collided gently with hers. "Good," he whispered, smiling madly. "Oh, good. I'm glad."

"I'm glad, too."

Then he took the ring out of the velvet box and took Katia's hand and placed the ring on her finger.

"I think we should do it soon," Katia said. "As soon as we can."

"Are you kidding? Let's go right now," Tom said, laughing and wrapping his arms around her. He realized tears were running down his face.

"Right now?" she asked. "Well. . . right now. . . you smell very bad."

"Okay, how 'bout in ten minutes? Or maybe ten hours—I could use a little sleep."

Katia laughed.

They stayed pressed together in Katia's living room, and neither of them ever knew, or was able to explain later, how long they had stood there—it could have been hours, or mere minutes, or days. . . .

OLIVER APPROACHED THE UNMARKED

metal door of the Organization's headquarters. He stood there for a moment, waving

Organization of One

impatiently at the hidden camera, and after a brief pause the door buzzed open.

When he got to the fourth floor, the doors opened and he stepped out into a cavernous, well-lit room. There were lavish Oriental carpets covering the stone floor. The ceiling was very high, with recessed sky-lights. Banks of computer monitors were inset into one high wall. They all were turned on—each showed a different surveillance view. Many showed the outside of the building; others were connected by satellite to cameras and transmitters in various places around the globe. There was a large antique samovar to one side and a table with a lavish selection of vodkas.

Oliver knew the place by heart—he had been here many, many times over the past month. And the so-called state-of-the-art surveillance teams belonging to the CIA had never discovered this place or figured out what Oliver was doing with his spare time because, thanks to the First Principle, he had won Rodriguez back.

"Hello, my friend," Nikolai said warmly, stepping forward. He wore a black turtleneck and brown trousers and held a glass of vodka. "Come, have a drink and tell me of the evening's exploits. I am dying to know how things have gone."

"Things are going well," Oliver marveled. He was on his way to the bar, where he poured himself a vodka and added a lime. "The plan worked perfectly. What?"

Nikolai was frowning in sour distaste. He gestured toward Oliver's drink. "That is what the Cossacks in

Leningrad do—pollute the vodka with *fruit*. It is not civilized."

"Well, that's the way I like it," Oliver said impatiently. "Nikolai, I can see this plan is really going to succeed."

"Just so. Come! Tell me of your evening," Nikolai said. There were two leather chairs near the wall of television monitors. Nikolai sat down in one of them, leaning forward and listening expectedly. "It seems to me that everything went quite well."

"I'll tell you, Nikolai, it was incredible," Oliver said truthfully. He had taken a swig of vodka—it was his first drink of the evening, and it went right to his head. "The plan worked. After we left you, we took a cab down to her apartment—"

"Yes? Yes? Go on, my friend."

"—and she invited me inside!" Oliver was reliving the moment in his head. Now that he could relax and think about it, he was even more impressed with the strategy and its positive results. "Nikolai, she actually invited me inside! It was all I could do not to accept."

"You are winning her back," Nikolai said, brushing his red hair away from his face. "The First Principle is demonstrated conclusively, is it not?"

"What about the surveillance team? Did they finish their work in time?"

"Oh, yes," Nikolai said. "Leonov called earlier on the satellite transceiver. While we were getting in position outside the restaurant, they successfully infiltrated

Katia's apartment and installed their sound equipment. I am expecting their report."

"Good, good," Oliver said distractedly, walking over to refill his vodka glass. "As soon as we can get accurate information about her—"

Oliver stopped talking because he had suddenly heard a familiar sound—the buzzing of a remote transceiver. He waited as Nikolai went over and picked up the handset.

"*Da,*" Nikolai said into the small device. Oliver could barely hear voices at the other end. "*Da,*" Nikolai said again. He covered the earpiece, whispering to Oliver. "It is Leonov—the equipment is in place. He has been monitoring activity in Katia's apartment."

"Good," Oliver said. The sooner all their surveillance systems were working, the better. It wouldn't take long for—

Oliver suddenly stopped thinking about the surveillance systems. He stopped because he was watching Nikolai's face. He could see the Russian's ugly features darkening into a frown as he listened to the transceiver. "*Niet, niet,*" Nikolai was muttering as he listened. Oliver stood there, watching, the glass of vodka forgotten in his hand. Finally Nikolai reached up, weakly, to shut the transceiver off. He slowly lowered it, an ashen look on his face.

"*What?*" Oliver said. A wild sense of dread was coming over him. "What? What is it?"

"I think you had better sit down," Nikolai said heavily.

"What?" Oliver was walking toward him. "Damn it, Nikolai—tell me what happened!"

"Twenty minutes ago," Nikolai said, "Thomas Moore arrived at Katia's house."

Here it comes, Oliver thought, stumbling toward one of the leather chairs. Nikolai was right—he had to sit down. *Here comes the bad news.*

"After some sort of verbal dispute, she let him in," Nikolai went on.

"And?"

"At eleven-forty, Moore proposed marriage," Nikolai said. "And Katia has accepted. They—ah—did not speak for a few minutes and then began making wedding plans. Apparently they are to be married within a month."

Oliver felt the world growing dark again. The entire room seemed to be blackening, like a burning sheet of paper.

But something else happened instead. Something happened inside Oliver's mind at that moment. In the midst of his rage a new emotion washed over him. It was a difficult feeling to understand—it felt like a soothing calm, but it energized him, excited him, at the same time.

Oliver marveled at what had happened in that moment—the moment that Nikolai told him about Katia and Tom. His dark fury almost defeated him—and then it burned him clean. It was like a bright, clear understanding of the world came into his eyes right then. He was standing on the Oriental carpet in the

Organization's New York command center, holding the forgotten glass of vodka, feeling a new, calculating certainty overtake him.

The First Principle. . . it was just another lie. Had he believed it was a law of nature that somehow could work to Nikolai's advantage and Oliver's at the same time? Had he really been that gullible, that naive? In the end, whether he believed in Tom, or in the CIA, or in Nikolai, wasn't it all the same thing? Following someone else's orders and trusting them to look after you?

Oliver's rage melted away.

Gazing levelly at Nikolai, breathing calmly, Oliver made up his mind, right then, about what he was going to do. He was going to trust nobody but himself. He was going to abandon the First Principle, the Organization— throw away the weak allegiance he'd had to others his entire life. Only on his own could he be truly powerful. From now on, he was an "Organization" of one man. Nikolai and his "important people" could get lost.

And Katia would be his.

That was the secret—he really could get the girl of his dreams if he threw away everything else.

Just wait, Tom, Oliver thought calmly. He had already decided what he would do—and his very next decision was not to tell Nikolai.

I'm after you for real, now, Katia, Oliver said to himself. *Just wait.*

Katia played the words *husband* and *brother-in-law* over in her mind. Not that she would have **1983** ever guessed this about herself, but she rather liked the ring of it all.

Cut the Cake

KATIA WAS DRESSED IN HER WHITE wedding gown with the veil pulled back, dancing with her husband's friend George Niven. They were in the Empire Ballroom at the Plaza Hotel, near the corner of Central Park. The ballroom had enormous, gilt-framed windows that opened up onto Grand Army Plaza. Katia's wedding guests could stand in the afternoon sunlight, looking out across the wide, European-looking esplanade, gazing down at the old-fashioned horse-and-buggy rigs that brought couples into the park. The wide windows had been left open, so the warm, fragrant spring air was blowing gently into the ballroom. It was exactly a month after the night Tom had proposed and she had accepted. The ballroom was filled with guests, most of them in black tie. Katia wished her mother could have been there, but with everything that had happened back home, that was not possible. But at least Tom and Oliver's parents could be there. Katia had loved getting to know Henry and Alice Moore this past month. It had honestly been such a great, great gift to have a father figure like Henry. Katia was so delighted by him she didn't even mind when he went on for hours about computer programming.

The wedding reception had been going on for more than two hours—everyone had eaten; Tom and Katia had cut the cake. Now couples were dancing on the wooden dance floor that filled the center of the ballroom.

As George twirled Katia around, she stole a moment to take in the scenery. Tom and Oliver, each looking as handsome and polished as a model from a magazine ad, were walking toward her. Tom, her *husband*, and Oliver, her *brother-in-law*, that is. Katia played the words *husband* and *brother-in-law* over in her mind. Not that she would have ever guessed this about herself, but she rather liked the ring of it all.

"Darling," Tom said. "Excuse me, George—I don't want to interrupt."

"What kind of a thing is that to say?" George scolded him, laughing. "Cut in, cut in—dance with your lovely wife."

"Actually," Tom said, leaning to kiss Katia for no good reason except that they both really wanted him to do it, "Oliver and I are going to have a drink."

"That's right," Oliver said, grinning. He leaned to put his arm around Tom's neck. "Just between the brothers." As far as Katia could see, Oliver had put all his jealousy of his brother behind him. It made for a remarkable transformation.

"Okay, but hurry back," Katia said. She had let go of George, pulling Tom closer; her ear was to his neck. "When I'm finished dancing with George, I'm going to begin saying good night."

"I think that's a good idea," Tom whispered in Katia's

ear. She felt a tingle of excitement as his lips brushed against hers. Behind him, she could see Oliver waiting, looking in the other direction. "Shall I meet you upstairs? Remember that we're in the honeymoon suite—room 712."

"I remember," Katia whispered back.

"Milady, may I have what's left of this dance?" George said. He was still waiting.

"Sorry, George," Tom said, leaning to clap him on the shoulder. "Oliver? Shall we?"

"Sure," Oliver said, leading him off the dance floor toward the edge of the enormous Empire Ballroom. "Come upstairs—I've got a minibar up there," Oliver said to Tom. Katia could hear them as they walked away and delighted herself in the knowledge that they had finally worked things out between them.

THE ELEVATOR ROSE UP THE CENTER

Spinning of the Plaza Hotel. Oliver and Tom stood side by side, alone in the elevator. The sounds of the wedding party grew fainter and fainter as they hummed upward. Tom was thinking about Katia and how little he enjoyed leaving her behind, in another room. But at the same time, there were certain moments when brothers had to be alone with each other. Tom was grateful to Oliver for inviting him away. It gave him a strong sense of warmth toward his brother, despite all the strain of the past few months.

And he would be seeing Katia soon enough, he thought excitedly.

The door chimed as the elevator arrived on the fourth floor. The gold-framed doors slid open to reveal a wide, red-carpeted hallway.

The corridor was quiet. "This way," Oliver said. They got to Oliver's door. Oliver unlocked it and pushed it open. It was dazzlingly bright inside his room. "I've got your favorite," Oliver said from over at the bar. There were buckets of ice, clean glasses, and rows of bottles, backlit by the bar—Oliver was holding up a bottle of Loch Dhu single-malt scotch. "Want some of this?"

"Sure—thanks," Tom said, walking over

"Here's to Katia," Oliver said, "finding her true love."

"I'll drink to that," Tom said. The brothers nodded, and each sipped their scotch. Oliver grimaced.

"I'm not partial to scotch," Oliver said. He was waving his hand, welcoming Tom into the suite's sitting area—there were stuffed red velvet chairs and a glass coffee table. "Sit down, Tom. Let's have a talk, you and me."

"So you're married now," Oliver said. He had put down his glass. "After two and a half months of romance—"

"Well, just one, actually," Tom said. He smiled at Oliver.

"You can call it one if you want," Oliver said, a bit sternly. "If you still want to pretend you were writing your *thesis* all that time."

"What? I *was* writing my thesis, Oliver," Tom said. He was starting to feel dizzy; the Scotch must be getting to him. "What are you talking about?"

"Nothing," Oliver said. "Nothing at all."

Tom was wondering where the conversation was going. He couldn't tell anything from Oliver's facial expression, and his head was spinning. Could he really be drunk from two sips of scotch?

"Forgiveness is a great thing, isn't it?" Oliver said expansively. "It's a gift—something one should never take for granted because it isn't always given. I mean, what if we *didn't* forgive each other, Tom? What would that mean?"

"Um—what?" Now Tom was completely lost.

"Well, what if I decided that there was something you'd done to me that was dishonest? Or unfair? What if that happened?"

Tom didn't like this line of conversation, he realized. At least, as far as he could tell.

"But that would be okay, too," Oliver said. He was smiling broadly. "Because unfairness can be fixed, Tom. Injustice can be righted. It's really the essential step for letting bygones be bygones. Don't you think?"

Oliver stood up, walked over to Tom, and took the drink easily out of his hand.

"I'm making another toast," Oliver said. His voice

was echoing from somewhere far away—it was like hearing the distant call of an ocean-faring ship, making its way into the far distance.

Tom was trying to get up off the chair, but he couldn't move. His arms and legs felt like lead—impossibly heavy. His breathing had slowed down. He felt like he'd been drugged.

"To hell with the First Principle," Oliver said, raising the poisoned glass again. "I trusted that fool Nikolai for far too long. Now I'm doing things my way."

Tom was starting to black out—the room was getting dimmer, a tunnel in front of him. He could barely feel his leaden, worthless arms being lifted—Oliver was pulling on his sleeves, taking off his jacket. The sensations got dimmer, and he could barely feel the tug as Oliver drew his bow tie away from his neck. As he hovered on the edge of consciousness, he could just barely feel his wedding ring being painfully dragged off his finger—the finger that Katia had lovingly pushed that same ring onto, for the first time, only hours before.

"You just sleep now," Oliver whispered, leaning close, so that Tom could just barely make it out—it sounded like a faint yell from beyond a distant mountain. "I'll take over from here."

I've been drugged, Tom realized, lying on the floor of Oliver's room. *Oliver must have slipped something in my drink.* His head was spinning painfully. Oliver had left. Tom realized that his clothes were gone—he was in his underwear.

With every ounce of strength he could muster, Tom tried to move. If he could get to the phone, Tom thought desperately, he could call Agent Rodriguez, who was still down in the Empire Ballroom, with his backup men—and with his CIA transceiver. If he could call and alert Rodriguez, Tom thought, he could dispatch him up to the seventh floor.

But he couldn't.

As terribly certain as he was that he knew exactly where Oliver was going—and what he was planning to do—he couldn't move an inch.

KATIA WAS STILL WEARING HER

Family

wedding gown. Her shoes were off—after all the dancing, she *had* to take them off—and she walked slowly back and forth on the soft carpeting of suite 712 at the Plaza Hotel—the honeymoon suite. She had darkened the lamps so that only the evening light from the windows shone in. From up here on the seventh floor, the sunset was still fresh and bright. Katia was breathing a bit restlessly—she knew Tom would finish his drink with Oliver and return any moment.

Standing there, she allowed herself a moment to

utterly relax. For the first time in who knew how long, she was finally *safe*. If not permanently safe, at least safe for a while. She had a *family* now—the new, American family she and Tom would start together. *Had* started.

The wind from the windows blew Katia's veil around her face. At that moment, as the wind rustled against her, Katia heard a clattering sound from behind her that she recognized: the sound of Tom's key in the door of the hotel suite. Make that the sound of her *husband's* key in the door.

"Tom," she whispered as he came toward her. His bow tie, she saw, had come loose—it hung down on either side of his throat. He hadn't spoken at all.

"Tom?" Katia saw her husband's eyes glittering at her, reflecting the bright sunset, as he came toward her. "Tom, what—"

But he grabbed her arms and lunged forward suddenly, driving his mouth into hers. It was startling—there was a ferocity to the kiss that reminded her of what it had been like at the beginning. Back then, Tom had kissed her so urgently, and now it was that same feeling of desperation. Almost as if they'd never even been together like this before. As if they'd never even *kissed* before.

And then he was pushing her backward as he kissed her again and again, nearly gasping for breath as he propelled her toward the bedroom.

And he still hadn't said a word.

It was the
worst possible
conclusion to
the tragic
events that
began for   1983
her that
bright,
innocent day
in the Waverly
bookstore

Finally. A goddamn man. For the first time in my life, I feel like a man. Not some sickly boy who needs his brother to save him. Not some castrated juvenile waiting for his precious kiss on the cheek, but a *man*. A man who knew what he wanted and *took* it. *Took* what was rightfully mine. *Took* what has always been mine.

Standing in the shower, singing Bach arias to myself as the hot spray came down, I was still marveling at what I had done. Of what I'd had the *courage* to do.

I set a goal for myself and I obtained it. It is that beautifully simple. I obtained the woman of my dreams. I have taken her just as any other man in any other culture but this sickly, overly politicized one would have. It was our first time, in her bridal bed—and I even had the ring to prove that she was rightfully mine.

And it was worth the wait. Every minute of last night was worth the wait. But I'll never

wait again, Katia. You know that
now, I'm sure. Whoever said
patience was a virtue must have
never had an ounce of pleasure or
satisfaction in their lives. They
must have been young and sickly
like I once was. *Waiting* for the
pain to pass. *Waiting* for the
cure to come. *Waiting* for everyone else to solve their problems.

I've honestly never felt so free
and so clear in my intentions. Back
then, when I got sick. . . that was
when my weakness began. Falling
down in the lunchroom, the math
teacher running over. . . I can
barely remember it now.

Because standing here reaching
for the shower knobs, shutting off
the spray so I can return to bed, I
know my time of weakness has ended
now. I've finally grown strong
again—and I'm taking what is rightfully mine. And I must say. . . the
last night, and this whole morning,
have felt awfully. . .

Satisfying.

KATIA LAY BACK ON THE ENORMOUS

white linen bed in the honeymoon suite. She stared at the
shadows on the ceiling as the busy
Grand Army Plaza traffic flowed
past, honking, out the window.

Wedding Night

She could hear Tom in the
bathroom, showering and singing
to himself. It sounded like her husband was nearly
done. She smiled lazily, stretching out on the bed. It
meant he was coming back.

It had been a strange, intense experience, she
thought. Very unlike what she had come to expect
from Tom. Maybe she felt this way because it was her
wedding night? It reminded her of her first night with
Tom—there was no other way to put it.

The shower spray ceased abruptly. And then, still staring at the dark ceiling, she heard something else. A tapping noise. No, it was a knocking on the door to the suite.

Katia frowned in irritation. She was *sure* that she
and Tom had hung the Do Not Disturb signs on the
doorknobs. Hadn't they?

The knocking continued, getting louder and more
frantic by the minute.

"Katia!"

Oliver? Katia thought, confused. *What does he
want? Could he have picked a more inappropriate
moment to stop by?*

"Katia! Can you hear me? Answer me!"

In that moment she could hear the voice more clearly—and she suddenly recognized it.

"Katia, darling—it's *me!* Open the door!"

Tom's voice. Her husband's voice.

From outside the suite, coming from the corridor.

What—?

Suddenly Katia was wide awake. She sat up in bed.

The banging on the door continued, louder. "Katia! Open the goddamn door, Katia!" Tom's voice rang out. It was unquestionably Tom's voice. But if Tom was out there. . . then who was. . .

No.

A wave of anguish scraped across her insides as she understood it all in this seemingly frozen moment. She understood what she had just done—it was the worst possible conclusion to the tragic events that began for her that bright, innocent day in the Waverly bookstore. The act she'd performed with Oliver, on her wedding night; what she had done to Tom, to herself, to his brother, to her marriage. She felt betrayed and violated, but more than that, she felt like she had failed. Not just that she had failed Tom, for confusing him with his brother so obviously and so disastrously, but that she'd betrayed herself, that she'd let Oliver make a mockery of the love she professed to have always had for Tom.

We've all been betrayed. Disgustingly, unthinkably betrayed.

With a tremendous crash, the suite's gold-framed double doors burst open, their locks shattered. Splinters of wood sprayed onto the carpet. Katia flinched, pulling the bedclothes more tightly around her.

Suddenly Agent Rodriguez and four of his CIA backup men rushed into the room, their guns drawn. They were responding to a call Tom had placed when he finally came to.

"Tom!" Katia called out, stricken. And finally she could see him.

Tom came rushing into the room. The moment he saw her, his face changed—he stumbled to her, looking her over frantically. "Are—are you all right, Katia?" he stammered, reaching for her.

"Oh, Tom—" Katia clutched him, the bedclothes crushed between them. She began to cry. "Tom—"

"Shhh. It's all right." Tom held her. She didn't even know how he could touch her. She barely wanted to be inside her own body.

The CIA agents advanced toward the bathroom. "Oliver!" Agent Rodriguez called out. "Are you in there? We want you to slowly open the door! Don't make any sudden movements."

No answer. Looking over Tom's shoulder, blinking away her tears, Katia could see the bright thread of yellow light around the bathroom door. *Come out,* she wanted to howl. *Come out, you disgusting pathetic coward.*

Without warning, the bathroom door burst open.

Oliver rolled through it at tremendous speed. The agents were caught unawares.

"Look out!" Katia yelled at Agent Rodriguez. Tom flinched.

Rodriguez heard her. Just in time. He jerked his head to one side—and Oliver's foot whistled past his skull, missing him by inches. The momentum carried Agent Rodriguez backward, his shoulder colliding with the soft carpet.

If that blow had connected. . . Katia thought, horrified.

The next agent wasn't so lucky. He stepped forward, raising his gun and pointing it at Oliver's face. Katia had a moment to register as Oliver grabbed the hand that held the gun, pulling it forward. With his other elbow he jabbed at the agent's stomach while kicking him in the head. With a sickening crack, the agent was propelled into the air; he spun backward and landed with a loud thump near the foot of the bed, unconscious.

Two more agents moved forward, wary of Oliver's deadly kicks. But Oliver was too quick for them again. The first agent fired his gun—the shot was deafeningly loud in the close confines of the room—and the bullet smashed into the striped wallpaper next to the bathroom door. Clouds of plaster dust billowed out as Oliver performed a knifing karate blow that sent that agent's gun clattering across the floor. Without slowing, Oliver reached to his other side, intuitively knowing where to hit without looking. He knocked the other agent's gun from his hand with the same deadly maneuver—pulling the wrist, elbowing the stomach, kicking upward. This time Katia could hear the grisly crack as Oliver's bare foot smashed into the agent's jaw, sending him sprawling backward.

"*Stop him!*" Agent Rodriguez shouted. He recovered quickly, rising to his feet. "Come on—neutralize him!"

Katia watched Oliver spin through the air again—he was a dark blur, silhouetted against the bright bathroom light. The two agents fell loudly to the floor—she could hear them cry out in pain.

Oliver, Katia thought miserably. *Oliver, my friend. How could you?*

Tom was holding her more tightly now. But she was too numb to feel his arms. She felt like she was drowning. Drowning in shame and pure revulsion. She just wasn't sure who disgusted her more, Oliver or herself.

"Stand down, Moore!" Agent Rodriguez said. "That's a direct order! *There's no way out of here.*"

But Oliver seemed to know otherwise. He leapt to one side and sprinted for the broken doors that led out of the suite.

The agents had no chance of catching him—Rodriguez was still fumbling with his transceiver as Oliver escaped the room.

In the light from the corridor, Katia could see the haunting expression—the mixture of hatred and frustrated love—on Oliver's face.

Then he was gone, but Katia was certain that they hadn't seen the last of him.

Tom held her tightly as she cried, as if he wanted nothing more in the world than to comfort her, knowing deep down that nothing ever really could.

OLIVER HAD NINETY SECONDS TO GET

Ninety econds

out of the hotel. If he could do that, he was home free. It wasn't going to be difficult: he didn't seem to have set off any alarms.

He hit the subbasement. Opening a door marked No Admittance, he ran through a dark cement tunnel and into a small, barely lit room. There were several steel lockers—yanking one open, Oliver fished out a drab blue pair of janitor's overalls with the Plaza's insignia stenciled on the breast pocket.

With thirty seconds left to go, he wheeled around and spotted the aluminum ladder bolted to the room's wall. There was a *Sports Illustrated* swimsuit calendar pinned up next to it. . . and, in the ceiling, a trapdoor.

Smiling, Oliver pulled on the overalls, tossing the sodden towel away. Climbing the ladder, he banged his fist upward against the trapdoor—and heard a rusty creak as it gave. Another few shoves and the trapdoor swung open, its two halves crashing into cement on either side of the door's frame. Oliver saw the night sky and smelled cool fresh air.

He climbed the ladder onto the sidewalk, finding himself in a shadowed, fenced-off area just off Fifty-ninth Street. Passersby walked along a few feet away, but none seemed to pay him any mind. He took a deep breath of the fresh air, zipping up the overalls as he began to creep away toward the street. He was still barefoot, but nobody seemed to notice.

From his position in the shadows, Oliver turned his head and looked up at the bright flank of the Plaza Hotel. He could see its cast-iron pediments, shadows against the darkening sky. Counting up to the seventh floor, Oliver found Katia and Tom's window—it was brightly lit, and he caught a glimpse of wild shadows up there—no doubt Rodriguez and his agents trying belatedly to secure the room.

"Too late," Oliver whispered, gazing up at the room. "You missed me, Rodriguez."

"But *I* did not miss you, my friend."

Oliver jumped. The familiar voice had come from an inch behind his left ear. It was completely unexpected. At the same moment he felt a viselike grip around his upper arm.

Oliver turned his head. Nikolai stood right beside him, his red hair blown by the wind from Central Park. Boris, the gray-suited agent who Oliver had injured a month before, was also there, holding Oliver's arm. Boris leered at Oliver.

Oliver slumped. He was smart enough to realize that he was cornered. Whatever surveillance he had done, however he had pulled it off, Nikolai had planned this one well. Oliver had no doubt that there were more Organization agents hidden around the edges of the hotel, just waiting to stop him from running away.

"Get into the car, my friend," Nikolai said. Oliver turned his head to see a large black Mercedes parked right there, its engine idling. Through the car's dark, tinted windows, Oliver could see other armed Organization agents inside the car.

"You have done a terrible thing, my friend," Nikolai told him gravely. There was an unmistakable note of contempt in his voice. "You made some *very powerful people* very angry."

Nikolai and Boris were pushing Oliver toward the Mercedes' open door. Oliver's bare feet struck the wet asphalt as he was pushed into the gutter. "Wait," he called out, twisting backward to look at Nikolai as Boris propelled him toward the open car door.

He landed in the car and was rudely pushed against the backseat. There were two other agents in the car.

Then Nikolai entered the car, pulling the door shut and locking it. Oliver was trapped.

"Yuri," Nikolai started. He reached behind his head, tapping on the tinted glass partition behind the driver. The Merecedes' engine started. "Yuri is very important person." Nikolai went on. "And you have badly disappointed him."

"But your plan would never have worked," Oliver said in disgust. He could feel the Mercedes slowly moving, attempting to pull out into the traffic along Central Park South. "Don't you see? She would have married my brother no matter what." He grinned at the Russian. "And in the end, I don't care about your stupid plan. I've had the best night of my life—I've finally got what I always wanted. So what if your 'Yuri' doesn't get to 'win her back'? *I* got her back."

"Do you not understand even now?" Nikolai said sadly. The dim light from passing cars shone on his red hair and ugly face.

"Katia is Yuri's daughter."

It took a moment for Oliver to fully understand what Nikolai had said—and what it meant. And then a wave of dread hit him.

"What—what's he going to do with me? Where are you taking me?"

"It is best," Nikolai grumbled, "that you not know. Suffice it to say, it will not be an enjoyable journey, Oliver Moore."

The dark armored car sped off into the cold New York night.

It was worth whatever they do to me, Oliver thought. *It was worth it—for you, Katia my love.*

KENT: And then your brother disappeared.

MOORE: Yes. That's right. He was gone.

KENT: I seem to recall some further sighting—

MOORE: That's right. We managed to pick up Oliver's trail once, inside the Soviet Union, about two years later. There wasn't much to it—one of our operatives found out about an American who the Organization had stationed in Leningrad somewhere. It didn't look like he was being very well treated— one agent got a glimpse of him in a gulag somewhere, but that was an unconfirmed sighting, and the agent was shot soon after, so we couldn't follow up. I mean, we *tried* to find out more, but we couldn't. Later, as Soviet politics ignited, I kept looking for signs of him, but there was nothing.

He had vanished. The honeymoon suite at the Plaza Hotel was the last time I saw him.

KENT: Do you need a moment?

MOORE: No. I'm fine. There's not much to say. Katia and I got through it. I mean, we had no choice.

Now more
than ever
she needed a
massive dose
of that
denial that
ran through
her family
line.

GAIA WAS STUCK IN THE MOST
tragic state of stillness. She read
and reread the pages again, trying to fathom the sick, twisted
deeds of that speck of crap stuck
in the crevice of a sneaker that she called her uncle.

The Matl

Rape.

There was no other word for it. No other term that would describe it any better or make it seem any less of the god-awful despicable crime that it was.

The wedding night. . . You sick son of a bitch. Their goddamn wedding night. How could anyone even envi-sion such a thing? Let alone be so completely void of any remaining goodness that he could actually go through with it.

And what made it so much more unbearable was that Gaia already knew how her uncle had been punished for his revolting deed. . .

He *hadn't* been. Because she'd seen him alive and well and free here in 2002, with plenty of money and power and whatever the hell else he wanted. Totally unscathed. Not locked up in jail for the rest of his nat-ural-born life. Not begging for pennies on the street after the world shunned him for what he had done. No sign around his neck or in front of his house that read Despicable Rapist: Please Spit on Me. Nothing.

Her mother's strength had never amazed Gaia as much as it did at this moment. And her father's. The ability to just put that horror behind them. Because they had to. Because they couldn't let him ruin their lives permanently, as he'd so clearly intended to do. Because now more than ever, they'd deserved some real happiness. They'd deserved a chance to finally step out of his repellent black shadow and find themselves a little place in the sun for a while, like all people in love so desperately needed. Like Gaia had needed and been denied.

And who had robbed her of that God-given right? *The same man.* She knew that now for sure. Oliver, Loki, his name didn't matter. It was still the same man. The same man casting the same black shadow over anyone's happiness, anyone's untainted love story. *History repeats itself.* Again and again.

The more Gaia thought about how much she hated Oliver, the less she had to think about something even more sinister. More hateful.

She was doing every single thing in her power to block it out of her head, but there was really no point. Of course, she couldn't be sure. There was no way to be sure. It wasn't like her parents hadn't been sleeping together that whole month before the wedding. But when she did the math. . . her uncle had slept with her mother on the wedding night. . . and Gaia was born about nine months after that.

Enough. That's enough. She'd already indulged the thought too long. Made it too real. Now more than ever she needed a massive dose of that denial that ran through her family line. Denial. . . Her uncle had been awfully good at denial, too. Or maybe he *wasn't* her uncle. Maybe he was what he had always told her he was. Maybe he was. . .

Stop, Gaia. Change the thought. Change it now. Stop, she commanded herself once again. *Just stop it. Let it go, Gaia.*

She dumped the entire horrid line of thinking as best she could and refocused on the transcript in her hands.

But there was no more transcript to focus on. The only other thing Nikolai had left in the binder was a small piece of white notepaper. It was no bigger than a slip from a telephone message pad. And the only thing written on the notepaper was a number. *790.* But when Gaia saw the number, it was like seeing the first sign of light at the end of a long, dark tunnel.

This was nothing like the unexplained faint memories of the Soldiers' and Sailors' Monument. This was Gaia's memory at its most complete—its most fine-tuned. The number 790 had sparked an endless string of vivid images: a large yellow hutch on dark and creaky wooden floors. A changing table placed the perfect distance from the bed for long-distance jumping. A beautiful gray field mouse named Jonathan, who could roam freely through her room.

790 West End Avenue. The former Moore family residence.

The train ride seemed to take an eternity. Gaia's anticipation level was making the passing of time far too frustrating. Because honestly, when was the last time she could say she was "on her way home" and not feel like she was somehow lying? The apartment at 790 West End Avenue. . . that was one of the only two actual homes she'd ever had in her life. That, and the house in the Berkshires.

As she entered the building, she breathed in that specific scent that had simply meant "home" to her as a child. She now realized it was just the combination of floor polish and fresh laundry coming through the air vents from the laundry room in the basement. Still, it was home just the same.

"Gaia Moore?" A voice came from behind her, echoing through the lobby. She turned around and realized the doorman was looking at her quizzically, holding a large manila envelope in his hand.

Yes. Perfect.

She snapped the envelope out of his hand, thanked him, and sprinted again, leaving the glorious experience of reentering 790 West End behind so she could continue over to her next favorite location as a child—Riverside Park. Once she was there, she could bask in memories without interruption.

She found a private spot in the park—a small patch of grass surrounded by three different rather large rock formations—and dumped out the contents of the new envelope. And yes. . . exactly what she was looking for, another page from her mother's journal.

A baby! I have had a real live baby with ten fingers and ten toes and the most adorable little mouth and the tiniest little specks of blond hair and the world's biggest, most beautiful head. And I can say right now, with absolutely no reservations, that she is perfect. Tom and I agree. I have given birth to the perfect baby. In fact, she is so undeniably perfect that Tom and I have decided to name her after a goddess. The Greek earth goddess "Gaia."

Tom and I think there is already something unique about our daughter. Because when she entered the world. . . she didn't cry. Not one tear. Just a look of curiosity on her face. She seemed to be sizing up the doctor and the nurses, examining them like a thoughtful young graduate student in anthropology.

I suppose it was rather remarkable. It was as if she were already completely prepared to enter this totally alien land. As if she had been born without a fear or worry in the world.

Of course. . . somewhere in the midst of all this unadulterated joy and overwhelming elation, I suppose there was that horrid nagging question somewhere very, very far in the back of my head. And I'm sure Tom's, too. The doctors were pretty clear about when my beautiful Gaia was conceived. Tom and I both knew that meant there was a very real possibility that the father was in fact. . .

No, we don't think about that. Tom and I don't think about it. We're just glad that he's gone. Hopefully for good. I believe that. I believe he's gone for good.

She is simply too perfect to have come from him. I know it. I know it in my heart. Gaia has only good in her. I can see it in her remarkably calm eyes. So she couldn't be his. She couldn't be.

MOORE: Yes. . . [*Pause*] Yes, I knew that was a possibility. We were certainly clear on the two-week period in which she'd been conceived. And yes, the wedding night fell in that period. But Katia and I had been intimate together that whole time, too. We couldn't really know. There was no way to know. It's not like blood tests would have told us anything. We're a complete genetic match. And you want to know the truth? [*Pause*] I didn't care. And I told her that. He was finally out of our lives, and that was all that mattered to me either way. I loved my child so much. From the moment I laid eyes on that calm, curious face. No, before that. Before she was even born, I loved her more than anything else in the world. And that had nothing to do with biology. That had to do with love. And family. Gaia was my daughter, and she always would be. And Katia and I had never been so happy. Not even that night by the water in Battery Park. We had been given a gift. I think we'd been given a bigger gift than either one of us could really understand.

The world's calmest baby. It was true. But that was just the beginning. It started to seem like every day she was doing some new strange and remarkable thing. Katia and I had no idea what to make of it. At first, we would just revel in it. Revel in the fact that there was something so clearly special about our Gaia. It was a source of nonstop entertainment and awe. I mean, not only did the girl almost *never* cry, but she also never seemed to *mind* anything. She never minded being left alone in her crib at night like every other baby I'd ever seen. She never minded loud noises or huge dogs. She never even seemed to mind when she had to be punished. I had to teach her, you know. "Don't climb the stove, Gaia." "Get away from the electrical outlet, Gaia." "Never go near a fire, Gaia!" But every time I'd scold her. . . she'd just stare at me innocently and say, "Okay." That was it. "Okay, Daddy." Never crying, never running away. Never grabbing onto her mother's leg or hiding when she'd been bad. Just, "Okay, Daddy." And by the way. . . those "okay, Daddys". . . she was eight months old. She was talking at six months, walking at seven, and climbing at eight. But that wasn't all.

By the time Gaia was two and three, her "special qualities" had started to leave the realm of special. To be totally honest, her behavior started to scare us. A lot. We started to feel anxious all the time. Because we never knew what she would do next. With the kinds of behaviors she kept exhibiting again and again, we never quite knew how to keep her safe from herself. After a while I remember Katia started to keep a baby book. She wanted to have some way of recording all the incidents. We both felt the need to keep track, maybe to learn—to try and understand better what was happening to our daughter. I thought the baby book was a great idea.

GAIA DROPPED HER FATHER'S TRAN-

Spicy Lilacs

script on the ground and reached for the manila envelope, her heart pounding with anticipation. *Come on, Nikolai,* she thought, shoving her hand deep into the envelope. *You said you had everything. Prove it. Tell me you really had everything...*

And sure enough, her fingers latched onto a booklike object with hard covers and a spiral binding. Gaia tugged it out into the sunlight and took a long, hard look. And the moment she saw it—the moment she saw the picture of herself at four years old framed in pressed flowers, that familiar smell of spicy lilacs wafting into her nostrils—she knew she had just discovered her new prized possession.

Gaia's baby book. A beautiful spiral book, thick with photos and postcards and dried-up Scotch tape. Every page covered in her mother's handwriting, English this time, written in various colors of pen from all the years of different entries.

The book had clearly been a traditional baby book—the kind of thing you could buy at a stationery store or a bookstore and give as a gift at a shower or something. There were certain preprinted milestones at the beginning. *First steps, first word,* etc. But Gaia's mother had crossed out those milestones with a red pen and written in very different milestones. Instead of *Gaia's first word,* her mother had written, *Gaia's first sentence.* Apparently Gaia had opted to skip past just one word once she had decided to speak.

Gaia actually remembered that moment. Again her memory seemed to be functioning perfectly in all categories but the Soldiers' and Sailors' Monument. She remembered that her first sentence was, in fact, at six months—only because she had waited a month before she was sure that speaking would be the best way to go.

She remembered sitting in her high chair, watching her parents having breakfast. Her father had asked for the jam for his toast, but when her mother reached in the fridge, she pulled out a red jar that Gaia had been under the distinct impression was called "jelly." So she asked her mother, "What's the difference between jelly and jam?" And then she watched her parents stare back at her slack jawed like she was some kind of alien from outer space for asking a perfectly legitimate question. A question that, to this day, she had not really received a sufficient answer to.

The book began with a whole list of Gaia's very unusual firsts. First sentence at six months, first steps at seven months, running at eight. First time getting dressed by herself—one year. First math problem (9 + 5)—also at one. And then they really got interesting. First time using sign language—two (Gaia had learned it watching that woman in the corner of the TV screen translating for the deaf on *Sesame Street*). First word in eight other languages—two years, three months (the word was *injustice,* as Gaia felt that was one thing that was clearly the same no matter where one was).

Once the firsts had been filled out, Gaia's mother had begun to chronicle pages and pages of incidents that had obviously fascinated and concerned her and Tom a great deal.

Katia had written a small introduction to this part of the book. She explained how there were, of course, remarkable incidents that took place every day of Gaia's young life, but that she'd meant for this book to be a compilation of only the grandest examples of Gaia's awesome and sometimes terrifying behavior. This book, she hoped, could serve not only as a record for her and Tom, but also as a record for doctors and historians who probably, at some point, would want to know more about Gaia's "condition," whatever that meant exactly.

Gaia flipped through the book, reading up on more and more incidents of her undiagnosed fearlessness. She read about the Subway Incident, when at age two she jumped in front of an oncoming train to retrieve a crying girl's fallen doll. And about the Pit Bull Incident at age five, when she managed to subdue the wild pet by pinning him down until his owners put him back on his leash. Gaia had forgotten that her career as an ass kicker had started at such a tender age.

But by the middle of the book, she was only flipping blank white pages. She stopped and turned back, looking for the last page that had anything written on it.

The last page had only one little piece of writing. On the top-left corner, it said, *Age—6 years*. But that was all it said. As if her mother had been planning to write something about Gaia at age six but had never gotten to it. Everything was blank after age six. What was that supposed to mean?

She placed the baby book gently down on the envelope and swiped up her father's transcript again, searching for the exact place she had left off. And as if on cue. . .

MOORE: Well, it just kept getting worse. When she turned six, *she* changed. The way she would save people had started to change. It had started to become a little more. . . *aggressive.*

I remember taking her down to Riverside Park for an evening aikido lesson, and on our way back home, she overheard a woman being mugged in one of the alleys between West End and Riverside. I don't even know how she heard it, but she did. She ducked into the alley—this is six years old, mind you—and by the time I had caught up with her. . . *[Pause]* Well, I watched what she did to this mugger, and I was in shock. She'd undoubtedly broken his leg with one kick, and she'd probably cracked his ribs with another. Gaia finished off the mugger and then, when she walked back toward me, I could tell she was upset. Guilty, even.

Almost in tears. As if she knew she had used more force than necessary.

You have to understand, she and I had constant training sessions, but *all* my training with her was defensive. Everything in keeping with the laws of the *Go Rin No Sho.* Only as much force as necessary and just. But what she had done to that mugger. . . that was something else. Like I said. . . aggressive. And I just knew something was wrong. I couldn't put my finger on it, but I knew then and there. I knew the trouble with my family wasn't over.

AND SUDDENLY THE TRANSCRIPT

Psychobabble

ended again. What had her father meant by that last statement? *What* wasn't over? And *why* age six? What the hell had happened at age six?

Damn it, come on, Nikolai, Gaia moaned to herself. Why was he doing this to her? Why was he suddenly giving her less than half the material he had been giving her before? Was he just trying to see if he could frustrate her to death? Leave her hanging until she had literally hanged herself? Because if that was his goal, it was working. She huffed angrily and flipped the last blank page over, nearly ripping it out of the binding.

And then she saw that the transcript was *not* in fact the last thing Nikolai had given her. The last thing he had given her was actually lying inside the back cover of that transcript.

A postcard. The same postcard he had given her when this whole painfully cathartic history lesson began. And again she cringed, being forced yet again to stare at the Soldiers' and Sailors' Monument in rich and disturbing detail. Only this time the few memories she did have of the place were raining down on her in seconds, bombarding her psyche with horrid mental images. Yes, now that she'd been forced to remember that recurring childhood nightmare, she knew she'd never forget it again. It would surely haunt her for another year with all its little psychological dream symbols and self-analytical clues.

Gaia hated all that crap. Freudian symbols and psychobabble. The only interpretation she had of her dream was that it made her want to puke, and it made her want to cry. And the last thing she wanted to do was think about it for another goddamn year.

But it was too late. The images were already there, like sharp little spikes piercing various points all over her head: her father set against the orange sky, pointing his gun in his own face. Her mother screaming for him to put it down. Gaia trying to get to him before he pulled the trigger but totally paralyzed. Those cannons firing shot after booming shot. And finally her father killing himself with his own gun—blowing bloodred gaping holes in his own body.

What the hell did it all mean? What was Gaia's subconscious trying to tell her?

She flipped the postcard over. But this time there was no long typed-out note taped to it. This time Nikolai had left her one very simple and succinct message:

Do you remember? Try to remember now.

I'm trying, Nikolai, I'm trying. Goddamn it, what do you think I've been trying to do this whole time? Once more, Gaia racked her unexplainably dysfunctional memory for any images from that monument. She was thinking so hard, she was afraid she might just burst a blood vessel in her head. But that wasn't going to stop her at this point. *Six years old*, she told herself. *Try to remember six years old. . .*

But that was a waste of time. Straining her memory until she got an aneurysm wasn't going to do her any good. She knew she'd been left with no other choice. She knew what Nikolai was trying to tell her. However much she might have despised the place, however much she tried to avoid it like a plague, she knew where she was going now.

Of course. What would make her think that she'd get a chance to relive some *happy* memories for a while? Honestly. . . What could she *possibly* have been thinking?

Memo

From: KS

To: L

Subject now approaching 89th Street and Riverside Drive. Entering the grounds of the Soldiers' and Sailors' Monument. Please advise.

Memo

From: L

To: KS

This is *extremely* disappointing. N has been out of pocket for too long, and nightfall is only going to complicate matters further. He is trying to dredge up her memories now, and that is unacceptable. Dispatch a full team to that monument now. The time for subtlety has passed. Find N and terminate on sight. Repeat—terminate on sight. I will go myself if I have to, but this little trip down memory lane stops now.

For a moment she could see that the tower was really no more sinister or imposing than a giant sugar 2002 dispenser—the kind you'd find next to the salt and pepper at every truck stop diner in America.

AND SO HERE SHE WAS. STANDING

Cloudy Memories

smack in the middle of the last place on earth she wanted to be. In the black encroaching shadow of the towering white monument.

She could feel her teeth clenching incessantly. She could feel her stomach twist and her heart twitch. Every ounce of her being wanted to leave. She didn't want to be here. She'd never wanted to be here.

The monument itself was a large Romanesque cylindrical building, with tall white stone columns surrounding it and a huge white stone eagle jutting out from its domed roof. She tried to look at the tower now through the eyes of an adult, doing her best to shake off all the ghostly exaggerations and magnifications that always informed one's childhood.

For a moment she could see that the tower was really no more sinister or imposing than a giant sugar dispenser—the kind you'd find next to the salt and pepper at every truck stop diner in America. But it shifted back in her perception just as quickly, melding again with the ominous memories of her past and becoming far more threatening. So much so that she opted to turn away from the hovering talons of the stone eagle above her and face the white marble expanse that stretched out before her.

Below her were a few wide marble steps, leading down to the huge geometrically designed marble-and-asphalt floor. And just beyond that were the black commemorative cannons, aimed out at the water.

The sight of the cannons only brought back the few cloudy memories she had. The make-believe sounds of gunfire, and screams, and massive explosions she used to imagine. Sounds of war. She could still feel it on all sides of her, just as if she were a slender six-year-old child again, dwarfed by blocks of stone and the darkening sky.

She stopped for a moment in the center of the deserted concourse, feeling the wind spinning around her face, hearing it sweep by her like paranoid whispers. For a moment she considered the possibility that this, too, was a dream and that any number of horrors could take place in a dream without the slightest warning. Maybe that was why the place was deserted. Maybe that was why it grew darker and darker by the second, instead of every few minutes. But after a moment of consideration she knew that she was quite conscious and this was no dream. And the place was deserted because the sun was setting in Riverside Park, and New Yorkers would much rather be eating their dinners than getting mugged.

Six years old. It was echoing in her head now again and again. Her main objective. *Remember six years old.*

She swung around to the front of the cannon and

peeked down the dark barrel. And that was when she saw her next clue. It had been hidden inside the barrel of the cannon. A photograph. Not a particularly old photograph, just slightly yellowed around the edges.

Gaia pulled it out and brought it into what was left of the cold gray light.

It was like looking at a photo of a memory. Gaia, probably no older than six, and her father, standing together in the center of the marble concourse, having a training session. God, had her family been under the Organization's surveillance every hour of every day? What purpose could it possibly have served for them to have a picture of Gaia and her dad on her first-grade lunch break?

The picture showed one of those days exactly as she remembered it. Another sunny afternoon when her father would stop by her school at lunchtime and pick her up. He'd take her down to the monument, sometimes with a sparring partner he'd bring along, teach her a short combat lesson, and then get her back to school before lunch was over.

These were the training sessions she had always despised. But why? It made no sense. There was nothing she loved more than training sessions with her dad. She waited eagerly for the weekend sessions. She couldn't wait to get home from school for an evening session. So what was wrong with the midday sessions? And why was Nikolai giving her a picture of one of them?

She dropped down on the bench next to one of the cannons and cleared out her mind. She would make herself remember. She could do that. She could do it with sheer will.

No more screwing around. What was wrong with the midday sessions? Six years old, Gaia. Remember. . .

Holding him down
with his wrist and
then snapping his
neck back with a
full extension
kick would 1990
do "maximum damage
to his neck"
and "put him out
of commission
for days."

This Whole Stupid Monument

Gaia released the sound from deep inside her gut just like her father taught her to. Even if she was only six, she could still grunt like a karate champ. Straight from way down deep. From her "center," like he always said. Every move, every thought, every sound—everything from her center. She relaxed her limbs and mind completely, felt for the exact point of contact. . . and then she flipped her sparring partner straight over her head, letting out the loud guttural sound as she landed him carefully onto a blue practice mat.

"Good. Now let's try that kick I taught you," her father said.

Oh, no, not that kick. Gaia hated that kick. She hated it. That was another thing he only made her do at the lunchtime lessons. She turned her eyes away from her dad and shook her head slowly.

"Gaia. . ." he said, with the beginnings of a threatening tone. "Don't you get difficult with me today. You know I can't stand it when you get difficult; you *know* how angry that makes me."

"No," Gaia insisted, crossing her arms over her chest again and facing the glaring asphalt ground. "I don't want to do that kick anymore," she said. "Because. . . because it goes against all the stuff we usually say about fighting."

"Stuff?" he asked. "What stuff?"

"You *know*," Gaia said. She hated it when he acted like he didn't know what she was talking about. "All the stuff in that book. The *Go Rin No Sho*. Stuff about honor and being respectful to your enemy."

Her dad snapped back his head and blew out a long sigh. "Gaia, listen to me now, okay?" He knelt down to her and looked her deep in the eyes. She could still never believe how blue her father's eyes were. "I want you to forget about those books I gave you, all right? I don't know what I was thinking. Books like the *Go Rin No Sho*. . . they're filled with mostly nonsense, okay? Arcane and shortsighted nonsense. See, Gaia, in the modern world, all that *honor* stuff. . . that doesn't really work anymore. In the *modern* world. . . sometimes you need to be cruel in order to do what's right. Does that make sense to you?"

Gaia thought it about for a moment. "Not really," she said.

He smacked his hand on his leg with frustration and stood back up. "Do the kick, Gaia," he ordered. "Do it now." He signaled for the sparring partner to get in attack position.

"No," Gaia said. "I don't want to."

"Don't talk back to me, Gaia," he snapped. "You

know I hate that. Now, you get in position and you *do* that kick."

"*Why?*" Gaia spat back.

"Because I say so!" he shouted. "And *I* am your father! Now get in position... *now!*"

Gaia could see some of the other parents at the monument staring. She hated that. She hated when they saw her father yell at her like that. It was so embarrassing, and it made her stomach hurt. And he only did it at the monument. Gaia always figured that was because he was interrupting his busy day at work to come see her. Maybe that made him a little more tired and cranky or something. But still, she hated it when he did it in front of everybody. What she really hated... was this whole stupid monument.

"Fine," she mumbled to herself, feeling more angry at her dad than ever.

"That's my girl." He smiled. "Now, just give me half force, Gaia. We don't want to break our sparring partner's neck."

"Whatever you say," she mumbled. She took her position and waited for the attack.

The sparring partner came at her, and then she did just as her father had taught her. It was really a two-part kick. First she jabbed her elbow straight into the stomach of her opponent, grabbing his wrist as she did it and pulling him downward. And then as fast as she possibly could, she kicked straight up at his chin with a full

249

extension kick. Her father always said that when this kick was done at full force, the combination of holding him down with his wrist while he was doubled over and then snapping his neck back with a full extension kick would do the "maximum damage to his neck" and "put him totally out of commission for days."

Gaia completed the kick at half force, snapping her sparring partner's head back with her extended leg before she pulled his wrist the rest of the way down and threw him on the mat.

And the second she'd completed the kick, she leapt down to the mat and checked on her partner.

"I'm *really* sorry," she said, holding on to his arm. "I *hate* that kick. Are you okay? I only went at half force. Are you *okay?*"

"Gaia!" her father suddenly hollered from behind, grabbing Gaia's arm and lifting her back upright. "Gaia. You don't *apologize* to your enemy, for God's sake!"

"But he's not my enemy—"

"For our purposes, he is your enemy," he insisted. "And that kick was perfect. Don't *ever* apologize to your enemy."

Gaia's father looked down at his watch and saw they were running out of time.

Thank God, Gaia thought. *I want to go back to school.*

"All right," her father said, motioning to the sparring partner to fold up the mat and head back to the car. He leaned a little closer so they could speak quietly.

"Good job today, Gaia. And also. . . I wanted to tell you that you've been doing a great job with not talking about our little lunch meetings at home. Your mother is going to be *so* surprised when we finally show her everything you've learned! And you know what?" he said in a near whisper.

"What?" Gaia asked, whispering back with a smile.

"You've been doing so well lately. . . that you get a *prize*."

Gaia smiled excitedly. "What?" she asked. "What's the prize?"

He looked around them quickly and then leaned in even closer, practically whispering it in her ear. "We're going on a *trip!*" he whispered.

She loved prizes. And she *loved* trips. "When?" she pressed. "When are we going?"

"Next week." He smiled, squeezing her little shoulders and looking her in the eye. "So you might even want to pack a bag, okay?"

"Okay," she agreed happily, already imagining what she would pack. "Can I bring a field mouse?"

"Gaia," her dad said.

"Yeah?"

"I love you, sweetheart." He gave her a hug, and she hugged him back.

"I love you, too, Dad," she said. And she meant it. With all her heart.

Gaia was
apparently
no different
at six than
she was now.
Brilliant, **2002**
yes. But
still
somehow so
incredibly
foolish.

GAIA SAT THERE ON THE BENCH WITH

Supreme Rage

a horribly painful feeling at the very core of her stomach that was actually a physical manifestation of the new black thought that was forming in her brain. Well, less of thought than a realization, really. That realization: Gaia was apparently no different at six than she was now. Brilliant, yes. But still somehow so incredibly foolish.

She looked at the picture one more time, feeling her entire head begin to burn with the most embarrassing and shameful kind of rage. The kind of supreme rage that came when someone you despised with all of your heart had successfully made a fool out of you. The kind of rage that her mother must have felt that morning in the Plaza Hotel. The rage that came when you realized. . . you'd been face-to-face with the enemy. . . and you'd told them you loved them.

She began to rip the photo. She ripped and ripped until that humiliating, infuriating image had been turned into confetti to be taken up by the wind. She jumped up from the bench and stuck her head back down the barrel of the first cannon. No, not to try and blow her brains out, but to see if anything else was in there. Any more photos to confirm her overpowering suspicion. Any more transcripts to put the nail in the coffin of her realization.

And yes, not in that cannon but in the next, another manila envelope.

He knew what he was doing, that Nikolai. He'd put all her remaining clues inside the cannons. Because he knew that all the remaining facts she needed to hear would blow her away. Blow her to bits.

She ripped open the envelope and went for the next CIA transcript and disc.

CIA File # NIR-P4855J *[Incident Report]*
Rating: *CLASSIFIED*
Transcript Recorded—10/17/1990 02:32:14
Administrating: Agent John M. Kent
Reporting: Agent Thomas Moore

MOORE: The truth is. . . none of us would be sitting here right now if it weren't for Gaia's
first-grade teacher. If Gaia's teacher
hadn't been so good at her job. . .
[Pause] Well, I don't want to think about
what could have happened. I can't think
about that or I would. . . *[Pause]* I'm
sorry. I'm sorry.

KENT: Tom, do you want to take a break here?

MOORE: No, John. I want to finish this. I want
to finish putting this all down today
because I will *never* tell this entire
story again, John. Never again. Not to
Gaia, not to another superior, not to
anyone. Not for as long as I live.
Because I can't think about the things
he tried to do anymore. I can't let
myself think about it. So let me finish
this now. . . . Gaia's first-grade teacher.
I owe her the world. I owe her everything.

Because I didn't see it. I was too dumb to see it. Or too blind or in too much denial or something. I knew Gaia's behavior was getting oddly aggressive, but it wasn't until her teacher called me with her concerns that I decided to go to the school and witness some of this aggressive behavior for myself. And thank God I went to the school that day. Because if I hadn't. . . then I would have never understood the magnitude of the situation. And then it would have been too late.

Now Ms. Berger looked downright suspicious of Tom, as if perhaps he **1990** was suffering from some kind of mental disorder.

"I CAN'T THANK YOU ENOUGH FOR

coming in, Mr. Moore."

Tom and Ms. Berger

Misunderstanding

were seated at one of the child-size lunch tables in Gaia's school cafeteria. The faint sound of children playing was coming through the windows from the playground outside. Tom had positioned himself so that he could peek out the window at any moment and see his beautiful daughter playing with the other kids on the jungle gym.

"No, I should thank you," Tom said, turning back to Gaia's teacher and sipping from a styrofoam cup of watered-down cafeteria coffee. "Katia and I have been worried about Gaia, but I suppose we weren't sure how bad the problem was."

"Well," Ms. Berger said, wiping her oversized glasses clean with a miniature tissue from her front pocket. "I wouldn't have called you in if I didn't think Gaia was developing some very antisocial behavior."

Tom cringed. Even the smallest indication of Gaia being the least bit troubled felt like a blow to the back of the head. Within two seconds of this little parent-teacher meeting, Tom was already convinced that he ought to quit the Agency, accompany Gaia to school every day, sit next to her in one of those uncomfortable miniature blue chairs, and ward off all the potentially evil first graders.

258

"I know Gaia can be rather strong willed at times," he said, trying not to be defensive, but being so just the same. "I could certainly imagine her getting a little prickly if a kid was mistreating her."

"Well, actually, Mr. Moore. . ." Ms. Berger looked a little hesitant to finish her sentence. "I'm not sure Gaia is being mistreated."

"No?" Tom asked, trying to mask the inordinate amount of relief that gave him.

"No," Ms. Berger said, resting her glasses in her extremely curly hair. "I'm afraid that Gaia seems to be the one mistreating other children."

"Mistreating?" he asked, trying not to sound quite so incredulous. "That doesn't sound like our Gaia. I mean, I know she's been a little more aggressive lately, but we just thought—"

"A *little* more aggressive?" Ms. Berger repeated with a wide-eyed stare. "I'm sorry," she said. "I'm so sorry, Mr. Moore. That was unprofessional of me. But. . . I can assure you, at least here in school, Gaia has been more than 'a little more aggressive.'"

Tom peeked out the window and watched as Gaia tried to teach some of the kids the moves he'd been showing her. *That* was his daughter. Teaching the other kids.

He turned back to Ms. Berger. He wasn't trying to be disrespectful. He and Katia were concerned, and they were looking for any advice or answers they could get.

"A *lot* more?" he asked.

"A lot more," she confirmed.

"Well, how much is a lot more?" Tom asked.

"I'm sorry. . ." she replied, looking mildly confused. "I assumed you knew more about this."

"About what?"

"Well, about Jimmy Cantor's black eye? About Michael Putterman's sprained wrist. . ."

Tom stared at Ms. Berger in utter bafflement. She couldn't possibly be suggesting that his obsessively good-natured daughter was injuring six-year-old children.

"I'm. . . I'm sorry," Tom said with a slight defensive laugh as he straightened his posture. "You're not suggesting that my daughter has actually *hurt* one of the other children in her class."

"No, Mr. Moore, I'm not *suggesting* anything. I'm *telling* you," she replied, looking more stern. "And it wasn't one child, Mr. Moore, it was *two*. That's why I asked you to come in. Gaia has developed a rather. . . frightening temper. And to be completely honest with you, parents have complained that they don't feel safe having their child in a class with your daughter. I'm quite surprised they haven't called you themselves. To tell you the truth, Mr. Moore. . . I don't know that *I* feel safe in a classroom with your daughter. I do occasionally have to discipline the children, and I'm not sure I'd be comfortable telling Gaia to—"

"Wait, wait, wait," Tom interrupted. "There's obviously

some kind of mistake here, that's all. Or somebody's not telling the truth; maybe one of those other children was trying to—"

"There's no mistake, Mr. Moore," she insisted. "We all saw her do these things. The entire class. It was rather shocking, to tell you the truth. And I'm sure your daughter may have had her reasons, but that degree of violence—"

"*Violence?*"

"Yes, Mr. Moore, *violence*, pure and simple." Ms. Berger was beginning to look more frustrated and much more concerned. She placed her glasses back on her nose and began to size Tom up more carefully, as if she was perhaps searching now for *his* "violent" tendencies—the ones he'd apparently passed down to his daughter. "You know, I'd thought you would be a little more receptive to this conversation, Mr. Moore, I really did. I assumed all these lunches you've been having with Gaia were meant to help stabilize her, but apparently—"

"Lunches?" Tom asked, getting more confused by the second. "What lunches?"

Now Ms. Berger looked downright suspicious of Tom, as if perhaps he was suffering from some kind of mental disorder. "Mr. Moore. . . you've been picking Gaia up for lunch as much as three times a week for the past *month*. What exactly do you mean by 'what lunches'?"

Tom froze. *Oh God* was the only phrase echoing in his head now. He was now in a state of shock. . . .

But somehow. . . he'd also expected it. He'd always expected it. And he'd begun to expect it more. But just not. . .

Maybe he had it wrong. Maybe this was a misunderstanding, too?

"Mr. Moore? Are you all right?"

"I'm sorry, I think we're just having a massive misunder—"

Tom was interrupted by the sound of children hollering. But it wasn't the usual playful hollering. In fact, the entire playground had gone silent with the exception of the angry shouts of two children. And one of them was Tom's daughter.

Ms. Berger gave Tom a quick look that seemed to say, "I told you so," and then they were both shooting up from their chairs and rushing out the cafeteria doors into the school yard.

"Leave her alone!" Gaia insisted, placing herself between one of the bulkier boys in her class and a rather timid-looking girl. *There, you see?* Tom wanted to say to Ms. Berger behind him. *She's not being violent, she's defending a helpless classmate!* Tom and Ms. Berger both walked toward the altercation to break it up.

"Shut up," the bulky kid yelled.

"No, *you* shut up!" Gaia shouted back, leaning closer and closer to the boy.

"All right, that's enough—" Ms. Berger began, but before she'd finished her sentence, the boy had given Gaia a light shove to the shoulder to push her away. And her response almost put Tom into shock. . .

The slashing viper. It was unmistakable. It was something Tom had never taught, and *would* never teach, to his daughter. Gaia had just executed Oliver's patented kick. And she'd executed it with more precision than even Oliver ever had. Where could she have possibly learned that kick?

Oh God, no. Please, no.

But he already knew it. He'd known it before today. He'd felt it.

Tom suddenly fell back into real time—awoken from his revelations by his daughter's tears. Gaia was crying. She'd started to cry the moment she'd completed the kick.

Ms. Berger picked up the boy in her arms, who, thank God, was conscious. She carried him back inside, giving Tom a filthy look as she passed. And now it was only Tom and his daughter, standing fifteen feet from each other on the stark asphalt school yard.

Gaia turned to watch the boy being carried back inside, and as she turned, she saw her father standing there. And she ran to him, with tears streaming off the sides of her tiny face.

"Daddy," she sobbed, wrapping her arms around his shoulders as he picked her up and held her.

"It's all right, Gaia," he whispered. "It's all right, sweetheart, it's over. I know you didn't mean it."

"I *didn't*," she said between short, staccato breaths. "I *didn't* mean it; it just. . . I'm supposed to. . ."

"Shhh," Tom soothed her. "It's okay, sweetheart. Come here."

Tom lifted Gaia back down to the ground and walked farther from the school to the fenced-in perimeter of the yard. He knelt down next to her and looked into her shame-filled eyes.

"Sweetheart, listen to me now, all right? Can you talk to me?"

Gaia nodded her head, wiping her forearm across her running nose. Tom dug his hand into his jacket pocket and pulled out a handkerchief, which he used to dry the tears from Gaia's face. "There," he said. "Better?"

Gaia nodded as her sad eyes drifted out toward the street. He'd never seen his daughter look so guilty. Never.

"Gaia, listen now," he said. "I want you to tell me the truth. Who taught you that kick?"

"You *know*," she whispered, darting her eyes back toward the school.

"Well, tell me again," he said. He needed to hear it. Not that he wanted to.

She looked her father deep in the eye, like they were sharing a secret. "Come *on*," she whispered. "We're not supposed to talk about it unless we're at the place."

"What place, Gaia?"

"The Soldiers' and Sailors,'" she whispered.

Oh God. The Soldiers' and Sailors' Monument. It had been Oliver's absolute favorite place in the city when he was growing up. He used to love to train there every day after school. *Oh God.*

Stop acting surprised, Tom. You sensed he was back.

"Gaia," Tom said. "Just this once, *it's okay to talk about it.* Now, just remind me, when is our next little lunchtime session?"

"At the end of the week," she whispered. "Friday. For our surprise trip, remember? You're taking me on a trip. You *promised.*"

"Yes," Tom said, pasting a smile across his face. "Yes, I remember now, sweetheart. . . . Thank you."

That damn Oliver was so smart. He knew Gaia would never trust him if he just walked into her life and tried to steal her away. So he'd been working his way in day by day. In small, imperceptible increments. Imprinting himself as the father before he tried to kidnap her for life. Apparently he'd learned how to be patient during his time away.

"You didn't forget our trip, did you?" Gaia asked, looking disappointed.

Tom looked down at his sweetest of girls and wrapped his arms around her as tightly as he could. "No, sweetheart," he assured her, holding on for dear life. "I didn't forget. Don't you worry, Gaia. Everything's going to be okay. Friday. . . We'll be ready."

FINALLY, GAIA THOUGHT AS SHE sprinted down the block into the Soldiers' and Sailors' Monument with her knapsack fully packed (she had decided to let Jonathan the field mouse stay home). Her father had left her a message in her cubby at school that he

Dressed in Purple

wouldn't be able to pick her up at lunch but instead to sneak out just before after-school gymnastics was over and run the two blocks to meet him at the monument. She had barely been able to wait it out through gymnastics. For once they'd be doing something *fun* on a Friday instead of one of those horrible training sessions. She kept trying to guess what it would be. She was praying for the Bronx Zoo, but she would settle for Coney Island or even the Statue of Liberty. She jumped the two black cannons like hurdles as she always did and ran for the sun-drenched center of the concourse, where they always met.

And sure enough. . . there was her dad! Waiting for her with a big smile stretched across his square face. He knelt down toward the ground, spreading his arms out wide, looking just like that stone eagle jutting out from the white tower a few yards behind him.

Gaia crouched down her head and drove herself into his chest like a cannonball.

"*Oompf,*" he coughed with a bright laugh, wrapping

his long arms around Gaia's back and nearly squeezing every bit of life out of her. "There she is," he whispered in her ear. "There's my daughter. My one and only daughter. All dressed in purple, no less!" He laughed, taking a good look at her.

"You know purple's my favorite," she said, smiling in his eyes.

"Well, of course I know *that*." He smiled, too.

He ducked his head behind her back. "All packed and ready to go?"

"Yup," she said, stretching her thumbs on the straps of her knapsack. "Now will you tell me where we're going?"

"Well, I believe that would ruin the surprise, wouldn't it?"

"I guess, but—"

"Don't worry," he said. "You're going to love it. So, then. . . shall we? The car's waiting right out on the drive." He reached both of his hands down to her.

"Let's go," she said. She placed her bag in one of his hands and her hand in the other. And they turned toward Riverside Drive to begin their journey.

"Gaia!" she heard from behind her in a most familiar voice. *Mom?*

Gaia turned around, smiling, hoping that perhaps her mother would be coming with them, too. Maybe that was another surprise for the day. . . .

And sure enough, there was her mother! And she was standing right next to. . .

Wait. . .

Gaia was extremely disoriented for a moment, which was unusual for her. *For a second I thought I saw. . .* She turned back up to see if somehow he had managed to let go of her hand and walk over. . . .

Wait. . .

He was still holding her hand. *So then how can he be. . . over there? And over here? At the same time? Wait. . .*

Was she dreaming? She had to be dreaming. Her dad couldn't stand in two places at the same time. People couldn't do that. But Gaia was totally sure she wasn't dreaming. So then how. . .

"You're surrounded, Oliver," her dad said. The dad that was standing next to her mom, that is. *Oliver? Who's Oliver? My dad's name is Tom.*

"And how long have you been waiting to say that?" her dad asked in a mean voice. The dad that was still holding her hand. "You sound like we're twelve years old. Are we still playing cops and robbers, Tom? You still want to play spy games with me? Gosh, I'm flattered."

Gaia's mother and father had started to walk closer and closer to her. . . and her other father. *I don't understand it. Am I going nuts?*

At some point her mother stopped walking. She stopped a few feet away with a look on her face like she was suddenly incredibly sad, or incredibly angry, or maybe disgusted. Gaia couldn't really tell. But her dad kept walking, coming toward Gaia. . . and her other dad.

And before Gaia could put any of it together, they were face-to-face.

Her father and her father.

All Gaia could do was stare at them. What else could she do? She knew she wasn't dreaming, but she knew this couldn't be happening. So all she could really do was watch, with her jaw kind of hanging open and not a thing to say.

"Let go of her hand," he said. "You shouldn't have come back, Olly."

Her dad named Olly looked at her other dad with a really mean look. "Why would I let go of her hand?" he asked. "She's my daughter. You *know* she's my daughter, Tom."

"We don't know anything, Olly. All we know is that you became very sick. And you need help."

"Oh, is that right?" he asked, squeezing Gaia's hand until it almost hurt. "You listen to me. You already took Katia from me. You think I'm going to let you steal my own child from me as well? Well, then I would say *you're* the one who needs some help."

"That's enough," her dad said. "You're scaring the girl."

I'm not scared, Gaia wanted to say. *Just confused.* But she said nothing. She was still too freaked out, looking at her two dads.

"Don't interfere, Tom. I'm taking my daughter back. That's all."

"*No*, Olly. No, you're not. I just told you, you're surrounded by agents. Now let her go."

"Well, Tom. . . What if I told you that *you* were surrounded by agents?"

Gaia began to look all around her. She couldn't see any agents anywhere. All she could see was the Soldiers' and Sailors' Monument and the big sky hanging over the river, turning orange as the sun started to set. She looked back up at her dads. They looked like they wanted to kill each other.

"Olly!" her father shouted with frustration. "Just let her go. It's over! Can't you understand that? It's *over!*"

"Yes, Tom. You're right. It *is* over." With that, he reached inside his coat and pulled something out. . . a *gun*. He pointed the gun straight into her other father's face and. . .

"Gun!" her father shouted, stumbling backward as the father named Oliver began firing off his gun again and again and again. So *loud*.

"NO!" her mother screeched, running to catch Gaia's father.

"NO!" Gaia screamed, tugging on her mean father's hand. But his face had turned evil. It was the ugliest thing Gaia had ever seen.

And suddenly some one or some thing began to pull Gaia backward, farther and farther from her evil father with the gun.

"*No!*" Gaia howled, desperately trying to flail her

body around until she could break free. "Let go of me! Let go!"

There was so much noise all of a sudden. People screaming—everyone at the monument screaming. And explosions everywhere. Giant explosions. They had to be coming from the cannons. And even more cannons that Gaia couldn't see. Cannons out on the river in big ships, and cannons sticking out from the columns of the stone monument, and cannons aimed down from the roofs of the buildings on Riverside Drive. It was a war. Gaia was in the middle of a war. And her dad was going to be the first one dead. And then her mom would be next. And then Gaia. The whole family. Killed in this war on Riverside Drive and Eighty-ninth Street.

And finally Gaia could see the armies storming in from either side. An army of men in black coming toward her, firing off their guns. And an army of men in gray coming up from behind, firing more guns. Gaia had never seen so many guns. All of them coming together in the center of the marble concourse.

But Gaia didn't even care about the war anymore or all those explosions and armies. All she cared about now was her father. Not the evil father with the gun. But the father that he was trying to shoot to death. The good father. Gaia had to save the good father. She had to. If she could just break free. . .

"Daddy!" she screamed, trying to reach out to him. "Let me go!" she howled behind her. "Let me go!"

But a hand came around to her mouth, covering almost her entire face with its tight grip. She could barely even breathe. And all she could do was watch. She stood there, totally unable to move, and watched her evil father aim and fire, again and again, as bullets sprayed across her good father's side, springs of red blood erupting from his arm as the orange sky seemed to swallow him up.

Save him, Gaia, she ordered herself. *Like he would save you. Be a hero like him.*

The sweaty hand over her face slipped for a second, but a second was all she needed. That was the moment when she stopped thinking. She stopped thinking and she bit down. Hard. Sinking her teeth deep into the flesh of the hand before her.

He screamed a high-pitched howl of pain straight into her ear, adding to all the unbearable noise, but Gaia didn't care. She grabbed onto the wrist, stepped back, and flipped his entire body over hers, landing the blurry mass hard on the ground.

And then she took off. She took off like a rocket, launching her tiny frame straight ahead, pinpointing all her focus on that gun. Only that gun.

"*Hai!*" she screamed, straight from her center, smacking the gun from her evil father's hand with her flying kick.

She landed on the ground with a roll, jumping back up into fighting stance out of reflex.

"Gaia, come!" her evil father shouted. "We can still make it out of here. Together. . ."

Gaia wasn't moving. She only stared at him, narrowing her eyes. And then she relaxed completely, becoming aware of all that was around her, just like it said in the *Go Rin No Sho*.

"Sweetheart, let's go!" He reached for her arm to nab her. That's when she gave him the kick. Just exactly as he'd taught her.

His hand came close enough, and she latched onto his wrist, jabbing her elbow straight into his stomach with every ounce of strength her six-year-old muscles could give. And then like lightning, the right foot shot his chin straight up, snapping back his neck as the leg extended outward. And then she pulled back down on the wrist and threw him down hard against the ground, dropping to her knee with her clenched fist hovering over his face, watching as blood leaked out from his mouth across the cold white marble.

And finally, there was silence. Total silence everywhere.

Gaia stood up slowly and looked all around her. They were all staring now. With their mouths slightly open. All of them. The men in black. And the men in gray. And her mother and her father—her good father—who was bleeding from his arm but alive. . . and smiling at her with that gleaming look of approval that she loved so very much. That she lived for, really. Gaia had silenced them all.

273

A moment more and the men in gray began to head back toward Riverside Drive, then the sound of cars screeching away could be heard from behind the trees. Gaia walked toward her mother and her good father as the men in black surrounded her evil father and scraped him up off the ground, but then...

"Gaia!" her mother screamed.

Gaia turned around, poised for another attack, but her evil father made no move to attack her. The only move he was making was to escape. He kicked two of the men in black off him and fell in quickly with the retreating men in gray, who got him past the trees and into one of those cars on Riverside Drive. The cars that were now all fading into the distance.

Gaia turned back to her parents and smiled. But as she looked at them, they began to disappear. . . . *What's happening? What's happening to me?*

Everything started to get really dim and dark, like God was turning down some big light in the sky.

"Mom. . . ?" she uttered as her legs went wobbly. "Dad. . . ?"

And then she had fallen to her knees. *What's happened to me? Have I been shot?*

"Gaia!" her mother screamed, coming closer. . . touching her head. . . looking into her eyes. Coming closer but sounding so much farther away. "Mom. . . ? Mommy?"

And then there was nothing but blackness.

And as he looked
up at her, his
wrinkled face
and his torso
now covered in
bloody **2002**
bullet holes,
her heart did go
out to him. In
spite of
everything.

So much of my life has worked in reverse. Most people in the world hate their lives because they're so afraid. I hate my life because I'm fearless. Most people wake up from sleep and realize that the things they thought were real were just dreams. But I've just finally woken up and realized that this thing I thought was a dream. . . was real.

Not a dream. A memory. A goddamn repressed memory, all this time. . .

No, I hadn't been shot. I was just experiencing a blackout for the first time. My father didn't shoot himself. That was just the twisted way my memory rationalized the insane things I'd seen at age six. I didn't even know I *had* an uncle. No one had told me. And those cannons didn't fire anything. That was just how my six-year-old mind interpreted all that gunfire. And I wasn't paralyzed. Somebody just held me down. For as long as they could, at least.

But I was right about one
thing. The Soldiers' and Sailors'
Monument might not have been a war
zone. . . but I *was* standing right
smack in the middle of a war. A
civil war, not within one country,
but within one family. The family
that was created when young Tom
met the even younger Katia. Jesus,
that one day. October 16, 1990.
That was the day all of our lives
changed for good. And of course,
being the idiot I am, I have *just
now* figured out that these transcripts I've been reading. . .
they both were recorded on that
very same day—one at the CIA, one
at the Organization—directly following that nightmare in the center of the Soldiers' and Sailors'
Monument.

Correction. Not a nightmare. A
reality. I'm going to do my best
to never confuse the two again.

And now. . . with that entire
repressed memory finally off my
back, the rest of that day is
finally coming back to me.
Everything that happened *after* my

blackout at the monument.

I remember waking up in my
mother's arms. She cradled me as
she carried me into this huge
metallic elevator. I could see
the fear in her eyes. The poor
woman had been totally trauma-
tized. I wish I had been conscious enough to let her know I
wasn't afraid. I think that would
have made *her* feel a lot less
frightened.

When we got out of the elevator my mother handed my semicon-
scious body over to two men in
lab coats, promising me with
tears in her eyes that everything
was going to be all right. But I
already knew that. I wasn't
afraid. She had to have known
that by then.

The two men placed me on a
huge metallic rolling stretcher
and took me into a room with even
more strange gadgets. They
started to poke me and prod me
with needles, and it was so damn
boring that at some point I just
fell back asleep.

So now I remember everything
there is to remember. But that
doesn't mean I know everything
there is to know. But there are
only a few pages left in the
transcripts Nikolai left for me.
So I must be close.

MOORE: I just hope these tests will finally tell us what we need to know about Gaia.

KENT: Well, we've got the best people working on her right now, Tom. The best.

MOORE: I think if we can understand it, then we'll know better how to protect her. Not just from all the sick twisted criminals of the world. . . like my brother. But from herself. Although she sure did an incredible job of protecting *us*. Gaia saved my life today.

KENT: You're a lucky man, Tom. And I wouldn't worry too much about your brother. I'm sure the Organization will be sending him away for a long, long time after today's disaster. Hopefully at least another six years.

MOORE: You know. . . once we're finished with all of Gaia's tests. . . I think it's time to move my family out of the city for a while. Maybe to the Berkshires. Someplace quiet. Someplace where I can just focus on my family. Focus on keeping Katia happy and keeping Gaia out of trouble.

KENT: I think that would be a very good idea, Tom.

MOORE: Maybe my brother has finally had enough of this war. Maybe now that Gaia has finally rejected him, he'll leave us alone. Maybe we're finally safe.

END OF TRANSCRIPT

MOORE: I'm *telling* you, Yuri. If Nikolai didn't have such goddamn sweaty fingers! If he had just held on to her a little longer, we would have her right now.

NIKOLAI: This is nonsense! I already told you, Oliver, I knew you were training the girl, but you did not make it clear to me what she was capable of. How could I possibly have been expecting anything like that?

YURI: Yes, Moore, I do not understand. You haven't been clear in your reports. Explain to me how a six-year-old girl jumps directly into a hail of gunfire without the slightest hesitation.

MOORE: I don't know yet, sir, but believe me, I am going to find out.

YURI: You will find out nothing, Moore. Because I am officially removing you from this operation, do you understand? I am sending you back to Russia, where you will be unable to completely sabotage yet another operation.

MOORE: What? What are you talking about? Why?

YURI: Why? After today's pathetic failure you need even to ask why? Because you have been an utter disappointment, Moore, that's why. The CIA was *right* to demote you. You are worthless! I send you in to terminate Enigma and retrieve my daughter and granddaughter and instead you nearly get my *entire* family line killed?

MOORE: No! Absolutely not. I refuse, Yuri. I *refuse* to be reassigned. Gaia may be your granddaughter, but she is also *my daughter.*

YURI: You don't even know this for sure!

MOORE: Yes. Yes, I do. I know it, Yuri. I know it in my heart.

YURI: Well, you are still off this operation, Moore. Your ticket to Moscow is waiting for you. I'm not giving you any more chances to accidentally *kill* my daughter.

MOORE: No. You *can't* remove me from this operation. You don't even see how futile your mission is! Katia is *never* going to love you again. She doesn't want to have anything to do with you, don't you see that? But I still have a chance to win back Gaia. I still have a chance to win back her trust.

YURI: You're a *fool*, Moore. An utter *fool*. You always have been, and you always will be. We knew it from the moment Nikolai fished you out of that tragic little bar. You were only meant to be a pawn, you idiot.

MOORE: You are the fool here, Yuri! And quite honestly I think *you* have outlived your usefulness. In fact, I think *I* will be taking over your *entire* operation, Yuri. All of it.

YURI: What on earth are you talking about. . . ? What the hell are you doing, you fool? You would dare to point a gun at me?

NIKOLAI: Oliver, for God's sake put the gun down. Have you lost your mind?

MOORE: *He's* the one who's lost his mind. I believe it's called senility.

NIKOLAI: Put it down, Oliver.

YURI: Pathetic. This is your most pathetic display to date.

MOORE: Yuri, I've grown so tired of listening to you! I'm taking over this operation as of today. And *you.* I am putting you out of your misery!

NIKOLAI: Oliver, don't—

[*Shots disrupting sound signal—tape time delay*]

NIKOLAI: An ambulance! We need an ambulance!

MOORE: More like a hearse.

NIKOLAI: What the hell are you doing, Oliver? What the hell—

MOORE: Nikolai, I need to know now. Are you with me or against me?

NIKOLAI: [*Pause*] Put. . . put the gun down. Please, Oliver. Put it down.

MOORE: With me or against me, Nikolai? It's a simple enough question.

NIKOLAI: *With.* With you, Oliver. Of course.

MOORE: Good. Then it's official. . . . [*Pause*] Attention, all Organization agents and employees. I am hereby running this underground organization. Full and complete command. A monarchy of sorts. If Tom thinks that he is the goddamn king of the world, then I will happily take on the role of king of the underworld. Call me whatever you wish. Satan, Beelzebub. . . [*Pause*] No. . . *Loki.* The Norse god of the underworld. You can call me Loki for now. But know this: In the end, after all is said and done, even my worst actions, even my most despicable deeds. . . they will all be performed for one reason and one reason only. . . to set things *right.*

END OF TRANSCRIPT

World of Pain

THE TRANSCRIPTS HAD ENDED. GAIA wasn't sure how long she stood there just listening to air until the disc stopped altogether. She was sick now. So very sick to her stomach.

She had never quite been able to tell tell just how deranged her uncle had become, but now. . . now she knew for sure. Now she had the discs to prove it. When she thought about it for another moment, she realized just how terribly *sad* this all really was. Yuri and Oliver. Two tragic men, destroying everyone and everything around them—causing such a world of pain just to regain some kind of loving family that they'd never have.

Well, on second thought, it *would* have been sad. If they hadn't been such sick murdering sons of bitches.

There was still one last note at the end of the Organization transcript. A piece of white notepaper even smaller than the last. Because Nikolai's note was so simple this time:

In the tomb. Now. We'll only have minutes.

Yes. Yes, finally! This was it. This was Gaia's prize for enduring this excruciating journey through her past. It was just as he'd promised in his very first note. Once he was confident that he'd shaken Loki's surveillance, he'd deliver her *all* the remaining information in those dossiers. *All of it.*

Gaia was already sprinting for the ominous monument, leaping the cannons just like she'd done as a child, taking the wide marble steps in one leap, and then she was there. Standing at the large black steel door of the monument itself—the door she'd never even wanted to look into. But as she peered through the filthy old window of that door, she could see him sitting on a dark wooden bench on the far left. An old and weathered man, with graying red hair and a tattered old tweed jacket with suede elbow patches. He patted a dirty handkerchief to his forehead again and again. He looked so old. Absolutely exhausted. Spent. But it was what sat next to him that interested Gaia the most. A thick black duffel bag.

There it was. Everything. All the missing truths. All the missing facts of Gaia's life that were still to be learned and understood. She'd made it to the promised land.

She creaked open the door and stepped inside.

Not knowing how to react to seeing the redheaded weasel in person. He'd meant so many different things to Gaia. He'd been such a menace to her mother, but he was also the reason her parents had met. He was practically responsible for turning her uncle against her father. . . but then again. . . all of her uncle's worst crimes were the things he had done on his own, against all the Organization's wishes. Most of all now. . . he was just the man who had given her back her past.

And as she walked closer to him, he actually began to smile in spite of his obvious exhaustion and supreme anxiety.

As soon as Gaia opened her mouth to speak to him, gunshots began to sound off like two tons of fire-crackers inside this reasonably small echo chamber.

Nikolai's eyes widened with terror as Gaia dropped and rolled to her left, trying to spot the hidden gun-man. Before she'd had another thought, Nikolai had taken off out of the monument, sprinting for the con-course in spite of his old age and the heavy black duf-fel bag dragging at his side. Gaia rolled to the door and jumped up, leaping down the marble steps and following him.

"Nikolai, wait!" she hollered after him as his jog-ging became more and more labored toward the center of the marble concourse. "Wait for me. I can protect you! Just stop running!"

Nikolai froze at the center of the concourse, dou-bling over for a moment and laboring to catch his breath. He was simply too old for a chase.

"Gaia!" he called to her, gasping. "Now. We must do this n—"

And then the shots were hailing from all sides, piercing hole after hole in Nikolai's fragile old body. His entire frame shook endlessly from the barrage of bullets cutting through every inch of him.

"*No!*" Gaia hollered, sprinting for him with all her speed, leaping straight into the heart of the gunfire, just as she had done all those years ago.

"HOLD YOUR FIRE!" LOKI HOLLERED.

He was barking his orders into a black walkie-talkie as he watched from the bushes near Riverside Drive. He hadn't expected Gaia to leap straight into the line of fire, though he should have. After all, he'd seen her do the exact same thing years ago; why wouldn't he expect it now?

"Hold your fire, damn it!" he screamed again. "She cannot be harmed, do you understand me? The subject does *not* get harmed. Under *any* circumstances!"

"Sir, yes, sir," the voices came back in boxed tones over the walkie-talkie. "Holding fire, sir."

Fine. Good. Loki could breathe a little easier now. Because the essential task had been completed. Nikolai was dead. Now he just needed that bag.

Three

STILL BREATHING. NIKOLAI WAS STILL breathing. But barely. Each breath was short and desperate. Like it might be his last.

"Hold *on*," Gaia told him as she knelt down next to him and took his hand. She couldn't even tell if her kindness was just a reflex or if it was some kind of heartfelt compassion.

She pulled his wrist closer to check for his pulse, and that's when she saw it. There in the fleshy part of his hand between his thumb and forefinger. . . a small, perforated circular scar. A bite mark. The deep bite mark of a small child. Yes, it was just as he'd said in his note. They had in fact met before at the monument, she and Nikolai. And now she realized why she'd never remembered him. Because she'd never seen his face. He'd been nothing more than the hand that held her back from saving her father.

But somehow, now there was no resentment. Maybe there *was* always a chance to repent. Maybe that was why she didn't despise him now as she thought back to the horrible thing he had tried to do that day. He was trying to make up for it now. And that was all Gaia cared about at the moment.

And as he looked up at her, his wrinkled face and his torso now covered in bloody bullet holes, her heart did go out to him. In spite of everything.

"I—I don't. . ." she stammered, looking up and down at his riddled near corpse. "I don't know what to do. I don't. . ."

"Shhh." He squeezed her hand tighter, coughing up bits of blood as he looked up at her with the strangest look of relief and satisfaction on his face. He had green eyes. She'd never known he had green eyes. "Shhh, it's okay," he whispered. And then he smiled at her. "It's okay now."

"But—"

"No, Gaia, *please,*" he choked out. "You don't talk. You listen now, yes? You listen. . ."

Gaia nodded, staying as silent as possible. He barely had enough breath left in him to make audible words.

"Gaia. . . don't feel any pity now. None. I *knew,* you see? I *knew* this would be my last mission."

"No," Gaia said. "You don't have to do—"

"*Gaia,*" he snapped at her with whatever strength he had left. "You *listen* now, uh? Just listen." Gaia nodded, holding tighter to his bloody trembling hands. "Now I know that mission is complete, you see?" He smiled faintly. His breaths were becoming shorter and more shallow every second. "Gaia. . . *all* the answers are in the bag. *All of them.* There are things in there *no one* knows yet. Not even Loki, Gaia. Not even your father. Plans. Plans that have been made for you, uh? Secrets about your future that Loki does not know. It is all in the bag." Nikolai's eyes were beginning to shut now.

"It's okay," Gaia told him. "It's okay, I'll stay here with you—"

"*No*," he insisted between breaths. "No, you don't stay here with me, Gaia. You take the bag and you *go*. *Now*, you understand? You go *now*. Don't let history repeat itself. Put an end to this war, Gaia. . . ."

All that was left to do was exactly what he had said. To take that bag of secrets and truths. . . and get the hell out of there.

Gaia reached for the bag, but a smattering of bullets began to rain down, obstructing her vision. Then a man in a gray SWAT uniform appeared before her eyes, snatched the precious bag right out of Gaia's hands, and ran away.

The Concourse

"DAMN IT, I SAID HOLD YOUR fire!" Loki howled, nearly crushing the walkie-talkie in his hand. "That was an order! Hold your fire!"

"Sir," the voice squawked from the receiver. "Sir, we are not firing, sir. Repeat, our men are standing down, sir."

"What?" Loki barked. "Well, then, who the hell is firing those guns?"

"Sir, that is unknown, sir," the voice replied. "Repeat. The origin of gunfire is unknown at this point, sir."

Loki's eyes widened as he slapped down the antenna and darted his eyes through the bushes out at the concourse. *Unknown? What the hell does he mean, "unknown"? If my people aren't shooting. . . then who the hell is?*

GAIA DIDN'T HESITATE. THERE WAS

no more time for hesitation. She dove for SWAT guy's feet like she was taking down a wild pit bull. The moment she'd made contact, she leaned hard into his knees and dragged him down to the ground, snatching the black bag from his hands.

Well-Traine Fighting Machine

But he countered. His first punch snapped Gaia's head back like a practice punching bag. And then his follow-up kick punctured her gut like a steel girder had just struck her. But that only made Gaia mad.

She relaxed her limbs and waited for his next kick.

And when she sensed the foot about to collide with her chin, she ducked right, letting him fall flat on the ground before jabbing her elbow straight down into the center of his spine.

"*Ugh!*" he cried out as she leapt back to her feet. She reached again for the bag, but he surprised her with a sweep kick that knocked her back to the ground. He wasn't giving up easy. She was going to have put him out of commission just for the time being. The bag was the priority now. Not a good clean fight.

Gaia dropped back a few steps, relaxing her hands in a defensive stance as the SWAT boy jumped off the ground and stepped slowly toward her, trying to keep his guard up. Finally he stepped right where Gaia wanted him. Her entire body swirled left as she leapt in the air and kicked out her leg, pummeling the side of his face with a perfect roundhouse kick that sent his entire body into the air and back two feet. She took one last look at his body lying in a heap on the white asphalt, just to be sure he was finished. And then she turned back for the bag.

But the bag was now in another gray-suited man's hands, and he was running. Running too quickly. Running for Riverside Drive, where he surely had a car waiting, if not a series of them.

"No!" She groaned, gasping with utter exhaustion from the last battle. But she tried. She wasn't done trying. One more leap for anything—the man's legs, his arms, a wrist, an ankle, *anything*. . .

But it wouldn't have mattered. Suddenly the phantom gunfire was pushing Gaia farther and farther back from that goddamn thief in the gray suit who was stealing Gaia's entire life from her. And there was nothing she could do to stop him.

"*WHO* IS FIRING?" LOKI SHOUTED pointlessly into the walkie-talkie. "All teams report *now*. I want to know *who* is firing. I want to know who took that bag. I want details *now!*"

He stared momentarily at the device, giving his men half a chance to come up with something. He was looking to be impressed here. Surprised. And then the muddied voice came through.

"Sir, I'm sorry, sir, we have no sightings, sir, repeat, no intelligence on this matter, sir."

Loki breathed out a long frustrated sigh as he dropped the walkie-talkie down to his side and stood in silence. He already knew what had to be done. He just needed to give the order. He brought the walkie-talkie back to his mouth and did what was necessary. "All right, retreat," he announced. "Do you read me? I want a full-scale retreat."

"Sir, yes, sir, packing it up, sir."

"Follow the man with the bag, is that clear? Those are your orders, to follow the man with the bag."

Loki smacked the antenna closed again and launched into a run for Riverside Drive. He could still spot something if he got there quickly enough, even if his incompetent men couldn't. He could still nab some kind of clue.

He landed on the paved street of Riverside Drive just in time to see the man in gray running with the bag, headed uptown.

"You!" Loki bellowed, pointing his finger at the man up ahead. "You! Stop!" But what had he thought that would do? Even *he* didn't have that kind of universal authority. A black limo drove up next to the man and opened its door as it continued to drive. The car rolled alongside him until he could throw the bag in and then leap in. Next thing Loki knew, the door had slammed shut and the car had doubled its speed with a nasty screech of tires. Loki took one last look. No license number, of course. Whoever they were, they were absolute pros.

Someone had outplayed him. The question was, *who?* He signaled for his own car to pick him up and ordered his driver to head back downtown, where he could lick his wounds and contemplate this most unexpected defeat.

Who would
possibly
think that
they had   **2002**
the brains
or the skill
to outsmart
Loki?

Deranged acts of love. That's really what it all comes down to. Generation after generation of deranged lovers, and fathers, and daughters. And standing alone in the center of the empty monument—my least-favorite place in all of New York—I can't help notice the irony of it all. All of us, past and present, searching for some kind of lover, some kind of family. And every one of us ending up either alone or dead.

But maybe I did find someone. I think maybe I found my father again. And I found my mother. So I know that this massive cathartic journey was not for nothing.

Yes, I think if Nikolai were still alive, I would be aching to tell him that he didn't die for nothing. That in fact he gave me everything I'd hoped for, whether it hurt or not. I wanted to know my mother. I wanted to know who had betrayed whom in that horrible love triangle. I'd wanted to know who the *real* Loki was.

And Nikolai provided me with the answers to all these questions, didn't he? I know about all the ways my mother was just like me and all the ways she wasn't. I know that my uncle is a sick, twisted son of a bitch who would betray anyone he could if it would serve his cause. I know that *he* is Loki and that I despise him with every ounce of my being. And I know now that everything he ever told me was a lie. All his stories about my fearlessness being some kind of chemical injection, part of some huge government conspiracy or something. Absolute and complete lies. My fearlessness was just as exactly as my father always told me. Just a freak occurrence that no one ever would or could understand, no matter how many tests they run.

And I even have one bonus. I know now how much I love my father.

I understand now, Dad. I understand how Loki has made it all so impossible. How it has been his one and only goal in life to turn me against you. I won't let that happen again. I promise you that. Even if Loki is my real. . .

Ugh. That's the one thing I truly, truly need to know. Is he or not? Is *that* what that strange look of concern in my mother's eyes was in the old picture of us hanging up by the stairs at George Niven's house? Did she know by then? Did she know the answer? Because I'm pretty damn sure that I'll never know it. I wonder if the answer to that question is somewhere in that black duffel bag?

I mean, what on earth was Nikolai talking about when he mentioned these "future plans for me?" What future plans? It was all in the bag. All those answers. I'm pretty damn sure I just missed my one and only chance to know those answers.

But maybe not. . . Maybe I'll have another chance.

They say that history repeats itself.

LOKI'S CAR SPED DOWN THE WEST

Try to Understand

Side Highway, heading back to his loft in Chelsea, where he could gather all the facts he had, collect all the reports from his various operatives, and try to understand what the hell had gone wrong today at the monument.

Who could possibly have taken that bag? Who would know about that bag or even *want* it other than Gaia or himself? It couldn't have been Tom; he was in the Caymans at the moment.

Who would possibly think that they had the brains or the skill to outsmart Loki?

HE ROLLED THE WINDOW DOWN JUST

Cemetery Before Nightfall

a few inches, hoping to let a little more air inside the rather stuffy limousine, and sifted through the top layer of materials in the bag, taking mental note of exactly what would be useful to him right now and what would not. There would be plenty of time to go through every single page later, but for now, he had accomplished the necessary task.

I am sorry, Nikolai. But there was simply no way I was going to let you give Gaia everything in this bag.

And there was no way he was going to let Loki see everything in it, either. There were still many things about Gaia that Loki knew nothing about. Things that would all present themselves in due time. And of course, there were the things that Loki still did not even know about himself. But why not let him suffer through that all on his own? He really shouldn't have dubbed himself *Loki*. He should have called himself *Narcissus*.

Let him drown in his own hubris, he thought, sifting through the bag a little further until he could find the envelope he wanted to be sure was still safely tucked away in it.

"Aha," he whispered quietly to himself, finding just that very envelope. He brought it up to his nose, breathing in that gorgeous scent of spicy lilacs. Unforgettable, that smell. Even after all these years.

"How are you feeling, Yuri?" his good friend Vladimir asked from the front seat of the limousine.

"Good," Yuri replied. "I'm feeling very good today, Vlad."

"Excellent, my friend," Vladimir replied. "That's excellent. So where to next?"

"To the cemetery," Yuri replied quickly. He had

known that was his plan from the start of this day. First the Soldiers' and Sailors' Monument and then the cemetery before nightfall. "I want to visit my daughter's grave. And then we can go home."

"Of course," Vladimir replied. "To the cemetery, then."

Yuri looked again at the front of the envelope, running his finger across her elegant handwriting:

10/18/90
For my dearest Gaia—
(Do not open until you are thirteen)

He pulled the letter out of the envelope and read through it once more. Just to feel Katia's presence that much closer to him. And then he folded it back up, placed it back in its aging envelope, and set it inside the duffel bag, along with all the other materials that Gaia would never be permitted to see.

"I'm sorry, Katia, my dear," he said quietly as he peered out the window at the trees flying by. "But Gaia cannot know everything. Not yet."

10/18/90

My dearest Gaia,
It has been two days now since we've had you down in the underground lab—God, it is so

strange down here. I don't know how they can go this long without sunlight.

They are still conducting their tests, and we are still waiting to hear just what exactly is so different about you. But Gaia, I have learned some other things in the last two days since that horrific nightmare at the Soldiers' and Sailors' Monument, and I want to share them with you. That's why I am writing you this letter.

I think, maybe, that I will not give you this letter until you are much older and more able to deal with such horrible things as this. I want that day at the monument to be the last ever day like that in your life. I think perhaps when you are thirteen or fourteen, I will give you this letter.

Gaia, your father and I will try so hard to make our family's life safe in the Berkshires, but we know that we may not be thinking realistically. Because the very plain truth is that something quite horrible might happen to your father or me.

Just know this. Know that your father loves you more than anything else in the world. More, even, than he loves me. Which is as it should be, I think.

But most importantly, the main reason I write you this letter is so that when you turn thirteen, if, God forbid, both Tom and I are not there to warn you, you will know these things for yourself. Because otherwise the consequences could be quite disastrous.

Gaia, you need to know that at some point in your life, maybe when you are still in elementary school, maybe not until you are a teenager, but <u>at some point</u>, a man will approach you, and he will look exactly like your father. Exactly. This is your uncle Oliver. And understand this: Everything he will say will be <u>lies</u>. Everything. And he may even try to convince you that he is your real father, but <u>this</u> <u>is</u> <u>not</u> true. We know this now, Gaia, as of just yesterday.

You see, while we have been here in this "safety zone" in the underground CIA headquarters, a superior of your father's, an Agent Rodriguez, gave us some confidential information from Oliver's CIA files. Yes, this is illegal, but these were very, very special circumstances.

This is what you must know and understand: Your uncle's medical reports indicate that he is <u>sterile</u>. He is one hundred percent infertile. Most likely the result of an experimental medical treatment he received in 1973.

You see, as Agent Rodriguez explained to us, this information had always been available to Oliver on request, but he never requested it. So he does not even know. He has no idea that he is sterile.

The point I'm trying to make to you, Gaia, is that your father _is_ in fact your father. And he loves you so very much.

So, for now, we will try to live the happiest lives we can, but of course, we will always be living in fear somehow. I suppose I am used to this. Always running from my father and now from Oliver. . . My God, that's not the life I want for you, Gaia. A life lived in fear.

I tell you, my sweet Gaia, all I can hope for you is that you can live your life with that same amazing quality that you have displayed so brazenly as a child: total fearlessness. Truthfully, if you can find some way to live your life without fear. . . then I will have everything I have ever wanted for you.

I love you, Gaia. And I always will.

Mom

> "Well, we could grind our
> enemies into powder with a
> sledgehammer, but gosh,
> we did that last night."
>
> —Xander

As long as there have been vampires,
there has been the Slayer. One girl
in all the world, to find them where
they gather and to stop the spread of
their evil...the swell of their numbers.

LOOK FOR A NEW TITLE
EVERY MONTH!

Based on the hit TV series created by
Joss Whedon

Everyone's got his demons....

ANGEL™

**If it takes an eternity,
he will make amends.**

❖

Original stories based
on the TV show
Created by Joss Whedon
& David Greenwalt

Available from Simon Pulse
Published by Simon & Schuster

SIMON
PULSE

"YOU'RE DEAD. YOU DON'T BELONG HERE."

SUSANNAH JUST TRAVELED A GAZILLION MILES FROM NEW YORK TO CALIFORNIA IN ORDER TO LIVE WITH A BUNCH OF STUPID BOYS (HER NEW STEPBROTHERS).

LIFE HASN'T BEEN EASY THESE PAST SIXTEEN YEARS. THAT'S BECAUSE SUSANNAH'S A MEDIATOR—A CONTACT PERSON FOR JUST ABOUT ANYBODY WHO CROAKS, LEAVING THINGS...WELL, UNTIDY.